Creepshow started.

It began with the screen going black. Then there was a blood-curdling scream and the camera seemed to be flying through the air while ghosts and goblins and witches and boggarts swarmed about. The scene changed to a big old house and we zoomed in through an upstairs window into this big dark old cobwebby attic. The show's host, a pale, black-haired witchy kind of a woman called *Walpurgia* sat in an old rocking chair, stroking a black cat with one long, skinny hand with long, curved green fingernails.

'Welcome back, dear viewers,' she whispered in a creepy voice. 'Welcome back to the weird world of the Unknown.'

Check out some of the other great books
in the Stacy and Friends series

Stacy
AND
Friends

Scary Sleepover

Allan Frewin Jones

Series created by Ben M. Baglio

RED FOX

A Red Fox Book

Published by Random House Children's Books
20 Vauxhall Bridge Road, London SW1V 2SA

A division of Random House UK Ltd
London Melbourne Sydney Auckland
Johannesburg and agencies throughout the world

Printed and bound in Great Britain by
Cox & Wyman Ltd, Reading, Berkshire

Papers used by Random House UK Limited
are natural, recyclable products made from wood grown in
sustainable forest. The manufacturing processes conform to
the enviromental regulations of the country of origin.

RANDOM HOUSE UK Limited Reg No. 954009

ISBN 0 09 926368 8

Hi, everyone. My name's Cindy Spiegel, and I'd like to tell you all about the long-awaited 'Spiegel Household Yard Sale'. My whole family was gathered outside in the sunshine, just longing to sell the perfect item to each and every visitor. There were literally thousands of bargains on offer . . .

At least that's what I was telling all our potential customers when my best friend Stacy butted in.

'Uh, Cindy, I don't think it's *thousands*, exactly.'

'Yes, thank you, Stacy,' I said. 'I really appreciate the input *right* in the middle of my welcoming *spiel*.

Like I was saying, there are literally *hundreds* of bargains on offer. Feel free to browse around – I'm sure you'll find something you like. Now I know this Yard Sale has been, like, several *years* in coming, but I'm sure you'll all agree it was well worth the wait.'

'I don't think it's been several years, Cindy. A couple of months, maybe,' Stacy chipped in again.

'Stacy, don't you have something to do over *there*?' I said. 'Look – Fern could use a hand keeping Lucky under control. Oh! And it looks like the clothes rack is about to collapse right on top of Pippa. Quick, go make yourself useful, while I tell the folks what's what around here.'

Stacy is my best friend, but she knows *nothing* about how to drive potential customers into a buying frenzy so they wind up forking out twice the moolah they intended to spend when they strolled by. (Fern says 'moolah' means money. She says you can also call it 'scratch' 'green-stuff' 'cabbage' 'the foldin' stuff' and 'bread'. Fern knows things like that. She doesn't know *much*, but she sure knows things like that!)

Anyway, back to the plot.

'We have bargains galore at the Spiegel Sale! Just browse around – that special gift is just waitin' to be found!

Rompers for your baby, dentures for your gran,
A pipe-rack for your uncle, a spare wheel for your van!

Rollerblades for your sister, a cowboy hat for
  Ben,
A map to show you where to go, a watch to
  tell you when,
Coloured pencils by the dozen, books for
  you to read,
You'll find 'em here at the Spiegel Sale – a
  gift for every need!'

How *about* that? Stacy and I wrote that poem
between us – but I learned it all on my own. It's
mostly true, except for the part about the false
teeth. We didn't have any real false teeth – but
we did have a pair of those chattering teeth that
you wind up so they go clackety-clackety-
clackety all over the table.

My horrid little brothers, Denny and Bob,
donated those from their huge collection of
dumb tricks and nasty Halloween novelty
things. You must know the kind of horrible
stuff that seven-year-old boys like to collect.
Flies in plastic ice-cubes and itching powder
and rubber snakes and wibbly-wobbly spiders
on a string and those icky splat things that look
just exactly like someone's been seriously *ill*.
All the kind of stuff designed *specifically* to irritate and annoy a cool and sophisticated ten-
year-old sister – meaning me!

Mom says I should love Denny and Bob

because they're my brothers. Well, I guess mom crocodiles must love their kid crocs – but I don't see why a sister croc should love her brother crocs when they're the most monstrous crocs in the swamp!

Sorry, I got a little carried away there. I'd just like to point out right here and now, so there's no confusion, that I'm not a crocodile, despite my big, dazzling smile and my swimming award. Neither is my mom a crocodile. Mind you, I'm not so sure about Denny and Bob.

In fact, while I'm telling you about my selling technique, how about this:

'Bargain of the week! A never-to-be-repeated offer that you just can't refuse. We have here a pair of unique and extraordinary seven-year-old boys. The perfect gift for the family that thinks it has everything. They can be used as doorstops or nifty bookends. Hang one in your closet to keep moths at bay! An ideal draught-excluder. Tie one out in your front yard to keep unwanted callers away. Only one careful owner (Mom). Take one for the rock-bottom bargain-basement price of ten dollars. Or take the pair for only fifteen dollars! Yes, folks, that's just fifteen crisp American dollars – you won't find a better bargain in the whole of Four Corners. In fact, I can guarantee you won't get a better deal anywhere in Indiana! And if you're not fully satisfied, we'll give you your money back and, hey, you can even keep the boys!'

Unfortunately, Mom heard me. 'Cindy, stop trying to sell the twins, please.'

'Yes, Mom.' Darn! There was a young couple who looked really interested in buying them, too! Oh well, I guess I'm stuck with them for the time being.

And now I guess I'd better introduce my pals who are helping me out with our Yard Sale. You've already met Stacy Allen – briefly. Stacy is my all-time best friend in the whole wide world. She's really smart in the most useful way you can think of – you know: like, she comes up with great ideas and fun stuff for the four of us to do, and she's the sort of person who makes life really interesting.

She thinks she's too skinny, and she thinks she has too many freckles, and she thinks her hair is kind of *blearrgh* and she has to wear a brace and she has a big dumb bimbo of a sister: Amanda the Airhead. But despite all these terrible, terrible afflictions, she's a really cheerful kind of a person.

And my other best pals? Well, way over on the far side of the yard is Fern and her puppy, Lucky. Fern is the smallest and the youngest one of us, but she makes up for it by being the noisiest and bossiest. She also wears clothes that look like an explosion in a paint factory. 'Psychedelic,' she calls it, whatever that's supposed to mean. 'Real bad migraine headache,' I call it!

I don't mean to sound like I don't like Fern, I like her a whole lot – she's really great to have around, but she's a little . . . uh . . . *loud* to have as a *best* friend, if you know what I mean. Having Fern as a best friend would be kind of like sharing a bath tub with a hyperactive walrus. Well, that's my opinion, but I guess Pippa would disagree, 'cos Pippa and Fern are total bosom buddies.

Next to Fern's clothes accessories table we have Pippa, who was in charge of the second-hand clothes rack. Sometimes I can't figure why Pippa and Fern get along so well, you know? Like, they're totally different! Awesomely different! As different as the most different things you could possibly think of.

Pippa is a total *intellectual.* That's Brain-Box to you and me, right?

Pippa's mom is a college lecturer, which is where Pippa gets her huge and throbbing Brain-Power from, I guess. If you ever need to know how to spell a really tricky word like *separate* or *receive* or if you have to know whether *absolutely* is an adverb or an adjective or whatever, then Pippa's the one to ask.

On the other hand, if you need to put up a poster in your bedroom, or if you have a flat tyre on your bike, then Pippa is the very last person in the world you want to get involved. Pippa is the sort of person who can turn pinning a poster to a wall into a four-alarm ambulance call-out. And she's the kind of person who can turn a tyre repair into the kind of disaster that makes Godzilla stomping through New York look like a picnic in a cornfield.

The reason all my pals were helping out with the Yard Sale was that Mom had promised us that if we put in a good day's work, we could have a mega-excellent sleepover party at my house the following weekend – as well as a small share in the profits! If we made enough money, I had my eyes on a really neat pair of red shoes that were totally to die for. If I could afford them, I wasn't even going to take them off when I went to bed. I was going to wear them forever!

Of course, the rest of my family were helping out, too. Well, Mom and Dad were helping out – Denny and Bob were just goofing off and messing around with their dumb little pals and generally being useless. (I wouldn't mind, but they were in for a share of the profits, too – and they weren't doing any selling at all! Lazy, good-for-nothing lumps!)

My dad was wearing his floppy old fishing hat. He just loves that hat. Mom had been trying to get him to get rid of it for the longest time. In fact she keeps hiding it in strange out-of-the-way places, but he always manages to find it again. Mom says he tracks it down by its *smell*!

Mom managed to sell our old vacuum cleaner to Mrs Dalziel. Mom can sell anything to anyone. She has a terrifically important job and she's a real high-flyer. You should see her when she heads off for work in the morning. Talk about power-dressing! The only problem with having a super-powered and important mom is that we hardly ever get to see her! She even works at home on her laptop, and sometimes it's like I have to make an appointment to say hello. (It's not really *that* bad, but she is kind of busy a lot of the time.)

Yeah, well, and then there were Denny and Bob. The mega-menaces! What's totally irritating about them is that they have such *innocent* faces. You know, they can smash the house to absolute wreckage and then stand there side by side with these big, goofy, innocent looks on their faces, and no one can believe that they would ever be capable of doing anything remotely naughty!

Huh! I could tell 'em different!

And, right on cue, in the middle of our Yard Sale I found out about their latest scam!

Those twins were going to have to die!

Let me explain exactly what happened.

I was on the refreshments table at the back of the Yard Sale. There were hand-painted signs up all over, pointing to *Free Refreshments*. We figured it like this: if you provide free lemonade and brownies, then people are going to stop off for a drink and a bite to eat, and while they're drinking and eating, they may well spot some item that they might like to buy.

That was cunning plan part one. Cunning plan part two was to site the free refreshments stall at the very back of the yard – so people had to make their way past all the stuff we had for sale if they wanted to be refreshed for free.

We sure did have a lot of stuff to sell. Dad and Mom had been packing the garage out for months. The thing about my folks is that they never throw anything away – and it doesn't take long for the garage to fill up with stuff that no one uses any more.

I guess what finally got the whole show on the road was that a distant great-aunt of mine died and Mom and Dad were what's called the 'executors' of her will. That means they were in charge of making all the funeral arrangements and stuff like that. (I wasn't too broken up about Great-Aunt Mattie dying – I'd never met her, believe it or not!) And the other thing was that Mom and Dad inherited a whole house full of stuff. Great-Aunt Mattie's stuff was in the sale, of course.

Like I told you earlier, Fern was in charge of the clothes accessories table: gloves and hats and jewellery and scarves and socks and shoes and stuff. Pippa had control of the clothes rack. Dad was covering gardening equipment and tools. Mom had household objects and bric-a-brac. Denny and Bob were selling off old toys and games and so on, and Stacy was in charge of the 'miscellaneous' table – which was basically everything that didn't fit anywhere else. ('Miscellaneous' is a Pippa word. We were going to call it 'Odds'n'Ends' until she came along.)

Well, we had a really nice, warm sunny day for our sale, and we were rushed off our feet right from the moment we started. There was a big stampede of people first thing who weren't interested in free lemonade, but who went through our stuff like sniffer dogs. Mom said they were probably hunting for antiques and for really valuable stuff which they hoped we hadn't noticed.

One guy asked about a pair of cute china dogs with black-splat noses and golden collars. He offered six dollars for the pair. Mom told him sixty was closer to the mark. He moaned and said it was a rip-off. He wandered off – but he came back ten minutes later and paid the sixty dollars. Amazing!

After the initial rush, we had a steady trickle of people. Friends and neighbours started to arrive, and they were all up for free lemonade and brownies so I was kept pretty busy.

Every now and then Dad would stroll up to see how I was getting along – and he'd give me a sneak preview of his money-pouch, which was filling up nicely.

A gang of really weird-looking punk-types showed a lot of interest in some of Great-Aunt Mattie's old clothes, and they ended up buying lots of things – including a really ratty-looking bright blue feather boa that any normal person wouldn't be seen dead within twelve miles of! (I was surprised Fern didn't want it.)

Stacy's sister Amanda mooched along with her Bimbo friends, Rachel, Natalie and Cheryl. I think they only came along to annoy Stacy and for free refreshments because they hung around making smart-mouth remarks and guzzling my lemonade and not buying anything.

My mom dealt with them in the end.

She came over while they were sprawling all over my table and talking about Eddie Eden's new hit single, and which of them Eddie would most like to date and grisly Bimbo-blabber like that.

'Hello, girls,' Mom said in her super-efficient way. 'If you have nothing to do for a while, I wonder if you'd like to help out.' She pointed over to Pippa's clothes rack. 'And you can have your choice of what's left at the end of the day. What do you say?'

Well, the Bimbos suddenly had some real important things they needed to do elsewhere. They were gone!

When there weren't any people in need of lemonade and chocolate-chip cookies (the brownies ran out by noon), I went to help Stacy.

'How's it going?' I asked her. I could see that quite a lot of the stuff was gone from her table – including the huge enamel elephant that weighed in at about a quarter of a ton and which I didn't think anyone in their right mind would want because it was so big. (Apparently it used to sit in Great-Aunt Mattie's front hall like some kind of weirdo guard-elephant.)

'Fine,' Stacy said. She pulled out an old tobacco tin and showed me all the dollar bills and small change stacked in there. 'Thirty-one dollars and seventy-two cents,' she said. 'I counted it twice to make sure.'

I pointed to a pointy-ended thing with a wooden handle and odd little cog wheels and metal bits sticking out all over. 'What's that?' I asked.

'It's a flange boddle scrooper,' Stacy said. She picked it up and wiggled one of the metal bits so that the cog wheels turned. 'See how it works?' she said. 'You put it in your flange boddle and kind of *scroop* it until the job's done.'

'What's a flange boddle?' I asked. Well – you would, wouldn't you?

'I'm glad you asked me that, Cindy,' said Stacy. 'Although I'm surprised that you don't already know. A flange boddle is a small but vital component of a wangle-tub. Without the flange boddle, the jelly won't go down the main pipe, and you can wind up with cherry stones all over.' She smiled at me. 'That's why you need to give it a really good *scrooping* with the flange boddle scrooper.'

I stared at her.

'What are you *talking* about?' I said. 'I've never heard of any of those things.'

14

'Cindy, you are just so gullible,' Stacy chuckled.

I caught on! 'You just made that whole thing up!' I laughed.

'I sure did,' Stacy said.

But the weirdest thing was that old Mr Groves came along five minutes later and said: 'My, my, a Matlock-Williamson bracket sinker – an original teak-handle Matlock-Williamson bracket sinker! My, my, I haven't seen one of those for ages!'

And he came right out and bought Stacy's flange boddle scrooper and went off with it like he'd just hit gold.

I had to scoot back to my stall to hand out some drinks to people for a while. When the rush was over, I strolled along to see how Pippa was getting on.

'Cindy, great!' she said. 'I have an idea – this rack would be better if it was a little higher – some of the longer dresses are hanging in the grass. Could you hold the end up for me while I climb in under and adjust the doo-da?'

It was an adjustable twin-rail free-standing rack from my mom's walk-in closet. It was a pretty hefty piece of equipment. You could make it longer and higher by unscrewing little knobs and pulling the aluminium tubes further out. I could see what Pippa meant – the longer clothes were flopping in the grass and getting crumpled.

I held the frame steady while Pippa clambered in among the clothes and started adjusting.

A little voice inside my head said: *Is this such a good idea? You know what Pippa is like.*

It was about then that the Pippa Jinx hit.

The rack shuddered and sagged a little.

'Is everything OK under there?' I called.

'Uh . . . up to a point . . .' came Pippa's voice, sounding kind of strained.

'What's happened?'

'The tube's come out of the other tube,' Pippa groaned from under the clothes. All I could see of her was one leg sticking out.

'Try to push it back in,' I said.

'I'm trying,' Pippa said. 'That's what I'm trying to do. What do you think I'm in here doing, Cindy? I'm trying really hard to get the tube back into the other tube. It won't go.'

'It came out – it must go back in,' I pointed out helpfully.

'I . . . can't . . . quite . . . oh! Oops!'

'*Oops?*' I said. 'What kind of oops?'

'I dropped the darned tightening screw thing. Can you see it?'

I tried to peer under the rack while still holding it steady. 'No,' I said. 'I can't see it at all.

Are you holding the thing tight?'

'Yes. Why?'

'Because I'm going to let go so I can get in there and help you out,' I said. But before I had the chance to get in there and help her out, the whole thing kind of collapsed in on itself.

'Yuuurk!' Pippa squeaked as she was squished under heaps of clothes. 'Yurk! Urgle!'

'I thought you said you were holding it tight!' I said.

'Gyaagh!' Pippa said. 'Arrgh! Nrffgrrk!'

Whump!

The clothes were in a big pile in the grass with aluminium tubing sticking out all over. The rack was a wreck. The middle of the pile struggled and fought and Pippa's head appeared. 'Well, thanks a lot, Cindy!' she said crossly, trying to get her arms free. 'Maybe you can help me when you're through *laughing*.'

Mom came over to help Pippa out. A couple of minutes later, the rack was fixed and Pippa was back in charge of the clothes, but this time with strict instructions to leave things alone.

At lunch time all us helpers had some sandwiches and Coke – but we couldn't have a genuine lunch-break because there were still people desperately in need of Matlock-Williamson thingamajigs and doo-das, so we couldn't desert our posts.

Denny and Bob's toys and games table was always crowded with kids – my little brothers seemed to be doing a roaring trade. The way things were going, they'd be able to buy the two things they really wanted most in the whole world: a Splaarg the Space Mutant Computer Game for Denny and a Splaarg the Space Mutant Space-zapper for Bob.

My kid brothers are really into Splaarg the Space Mutant. He's a cartoon character on TV – eight foot tall, green, and covered in wriggly tentacles. He spends most of his time zipping around the galaxy and getting into fights with Fnoof the Stinky – his arch enemy. Yeah, it's real *sophisticated* stuff, but the twins are totally into it. They have Splaarg bubble-foam, Splaarg posters on the walls, Splaarg pencil cases, Splaarg board-games, plastic model Splaargs with moveable tentacles. You name it, they have it. If a garbage can had a picture of Splaarg on it, they'd want one!

A small girl came strolling up to my table.

'Would you like a cup of lemonade?' I asked her.

'Ith it nithe?' she lisped – she had two missing front teeth. I felt kind of sympathetic – I could still remember when I only had, like, two vampire teeth on either side and a big, awful gap in the middle.

And, hey, do you notice how much your folks like to take pictures of you with your front teeth missing? 'Smile!' they say, knowing full well you'll look like a total dork! And then, years later, when you're ten, they'll get the photo albums out and everyone will say how cute you looked. Fern said that if having no front teeth is so cute, how come grown-ups don't have theirs yanked out? I totally agree with her.

'Yes,' I said. 'It's very nice.' I noticed she was carrying a pink box under her arm. 'What's that?' I asked as I poured her out some lemonade.

'A doll,' she said. 'I just bought it for two dollarth.' She showed me the box. 'Over there.' She pointed to Denny and Bob's table. 'It'th lovely.'

I looked at it.

I blinked and looked at it again.

I stared at it.

It was a Suzy Superstar doll.

It was *my* Suzy Superstar doll!

It was *my* Suzy Superstar doll from the box in the basement where I store all the stuff I still want, but which I don't have space for in my room.

Someone had raided my box! Someone – or some*two* – had sneaked stuff out of my special,

19

personal, private box and they were *selling my things without permission! Arrgh!*

I did my absolute best not to explode. I handed the little girl the lemonade. 'There you are,' I said. 'I hope you enjoy it.' I pointed over to the toy and games table. 'I just have to go over there and kill a couple of people,' I said. 'I won't be a moment. Help yourself to a muffin.' (The cookies had run out, too.)

I headed for Denny and Bob's table with murder in my heart.

There were half a dozen kids looking at stuff on the toys and games table. Denny was showing one boy how Buckaroo works and Bob was counting the pieces of a four-hundred-piece jigsaw because the little girl who was interested in it wouldn't hand over any money until she was certain it was all there. The way Bob counts, I figured she was in for a long wait.

Another couple of boys were sitting in the grass in front of the table and playing space battles with some really old Star Wars figures and stuff that had belonged to my dad when he was a boy. (I told you my folks never throw anything away!)

I put my arm around Denny's neck in a really friendly sisterly neck-lock.

'How's it going, Denny?' I asked.

'Great!' he said. The Buckaroo horse bucked and all the gear went flying. The potential buyer raced about picking the pieces up while his mom handed over the money.

'One hundred and sixty-one. One hundred and sixty-two. One hundred and sixty-three,' Bob muttered, moving the jigsaw pieces from the box and putting them into the upturned lid.

Denny opened a Splaarg the Space Mutant lunch-box and put the money inside. 'That's another three dollars!' He said. 'Bob! Another three dollars!'

'One hundred and sixty-four. One hundred and sixty – stop poking me, will you?'

'That brings our grand total up to forty-six dollars and eighty-five cents!' Denny crowed.

Bob went back to concentrating on the puzzle. 'One hundred and eighty-six. One hun–'

'You weren't on one hundred and eighty-six!' said the girl who wanted to buy the puzzle.

Bob frowned at her. 'Yes, I was!'

'You were not!'

'What was I on, then?'

'I don't remember. But it wasn't one hundred and eighty-six, that's for sure!'

Bob sighed. He tipped all the pieces in together and started counting again. 'One. Two. Three . . .'

I tightened my friendly sisterly neck-lock on Denny. I couldn't just rip his head off his shoulders in front of all those people, so I had to be *subtle*.

'Denny, I'm going to ask you a question,' I whispered into his ear. 'If you don't tell me the truth I'm going to kill you and bury your body in wasteland so that no one will ever find it in a million years. Do you understand me?'

'Yuurk!' Denny choked. 'Get off me.'

'I'll get off you when I find out how come there's a little girl over there at the refreshments stall with no front teeth but with a Suzy Superstar doll complete with its box which she just told me she bought from you.'

'Guurk!' Denny said.

'Hey, you stopped counting!' complained the girl who was interested in the jigsaw puzzle. Bob was giving me real guilty looks. I figured he was working out the best escape route just in case I went postal.

'My question is,' I hissed into Denny's ear, 'how come you're selling my personal private things on your stall?'

'Didn't . . . think . . . you . . . wanted . . . 'em . . .' Denny gasped as my arm tightened around his scrawny little neck. 'We . . . found . . . 'em . . . in a box . . . in the . . . basement . . .'

'I see,' I said. 'Are you referring to the box labelled *Cindy's Things. Private. Do Not Touch?*'

'No, not that box,' Denny said. 'It wasn't that box at all. Honest.'

Bob was sidling away. I grabbed his collar

and yanked him over towards me. The jigsaw puzzle box tipped up and the pieces went all over the ground.

'He-e-e-ey!' yelled the girl.

'There were ten pieces missing anyway,' I told her.

'Humph!' She turned and stomped off. 'Big rip-off!'

Denny tried to get free and all of a sudden there was a major tussle going on behind the toys and games table as both the twins fought like crazy to get away from me before I started handing out some top-grade revenge.

The table went toppling over. There was a yelp from the two kids playing Star Wars as all the stuff from on top of the table landed on them. Bits and pieces of games all went scattering into the grass in a big mess of dominoes and chess-pieces and Dungeons and Dragons stuff and a whole heap of other odds and ends that came spilling out of their boxes.

It was chaos!

But as the table fell over, it pulled an old towel off a box that had been hidden underneath. A large blue plastic storage box. Written on the side of the box in pink magic marker was: *Cindy's Things. Private. Do Not Touch.*

The box was open and it was darned near half empty!

When I had put that box in the basement, it had been crammed full of stuff.

Well, that did it! Now, normally I'm a totally calm, laid-back kind of a person who wouldn't harm a fly. But when I saw that the terrible twins had been selling off my stuff to help them buy themselves Splaarg the Space Mutant stuff, I totally lost it!

I went totally ballistic!

Mom came running over because Denny and Bob were yelling and howling and screeching. Everyone was looking.

It wasn't a pretty picture. My only real regret was that I wasn't able to kill them before Mom came racing up and dragged me off them.

Anyway, to cut a gruesome story short, Mom hauled the three of us indoors.

'What on earth do you think you were doing out there?' she panted. Mom always gets a little breathless when she is really, really angry.

I pointed a shaking finger at the twins. 'They've been selling my stuff! My personal stuff from my box in the basement!'

Denny and Bob stood there all meek and mild and innocent-looking.

'Is this true?' Mom growled.

Denny hung his head. 'We didn't know,' he mumbled.

'We thought she didn't want it any more,'

Bob added, looking really shamefaced. 'We didn't do it on purpose!'

'Like *heck*!' I yelled. 'The box had *Cindy's Things. Private. Do Not Touch* written all over it!'

Denny looked into Mom's eyes. 'We didn't see it,' he whimpered. 'We thought it was just old stuff for the sale.'

'Dad said for us to get stuff out of the basement,' Bob said. 'How were we supposed to know Cindy didn't want the stuff in that box sold?'

'No one told us,' Denny said.

Mom gave them one of her laser-beam stares. I could see that she was beginning to wonder whether it really had been a genuine mistake.

Genuine mistake my foot! No *way* was that a mistake!

The twins just stood there looking innocent and upset.

'We wouldn't have sold Cindy's stuff if we'd known,' Denny mumbled.

'She should have told us,' Bob whimpered.

'How could I have told you?' I hollered. 'You had the box hidden under the table with a towel over it!'

Mom's frown deepened. 'Is that true?' she asked them.

'I guess . . .' Denny said. 'But not on purpose.'

'The towel just fell on it,' Bob said. 'We didn't put it there on purpose.'

'You did, too!' I hollered. 'And now there's a girl out there with my Suzy Superstar doll!' I looked at Mom. 'You know I never wanted to get rid of my Suzy Superstar doll! She was just down there *temporarily*! All the stuff in that box was down there *temporarily*!' I snarled at the twins. 'That was why I wrote *Cindy's Things. Private. Do Not Touch* on the box, see?' I got sarcastic. 'I wrote *Private* and *Do Not Touch* so that people would leave it alone!'

'We didn't see no writing,' Denny said, giving me a really nasty look.

'Maybe it wore off,' Bob said.

'It was still there!' I snarled. 'I just saw it!'

Mom turned to me. 'Cindy, do you know exactly what was in the box?'

'Yes, I think so.' I nodded. 'Yes, I'm sure I'd be able to remember everything. It was totally packed!'

'OK, here's what's going to happen, guys . . .' Mom said.

The thing you have to know is that when Mom starts off a sentence with the words: 'here's what's going to happen', then you stand still, shape up and *listen*. Unless you really like

27

the idea of all privileges being taken away for a month or two – and that would only be after you had been chewed out for a very long time indeed.

'Here's what's going to happen, guys,' Mom said. 'Cindy – I want you to go and get your box. You can put it in the study for the time being. Then I want you to go back to the lemonade table and carry on handing out free lemonade.' She turned to the twins. 'Denny and Bob, you are going to set your table up again and sort out all that mess –'

'But Cindy knocked the table over, and –' Denny shut up when he saw the look in Mom's eye. Wise kid – for once!

'And when you two have gotten the whole shambles sorted, you are going to sell some more stuff, right?'

'Mphmmrumph,' Bob said.

'*Excuse* me?' Mom said.

'Yes, Mom,' Bob said.

'And when the sale is finished and you've helped tidy everything up,' Mom carried on telling us, 'Cindy – you can sit down quietly somewhere and make a list of everything that is missing from your box. And *you*,' she said, glaring at the boys, 'will spend as long as it takes tomorrow to go around to all the people you sold Cindy's things to. And you will get

Cindy's things back, and you will pay the people the money back that they gave you, and you will apologise to them and explain that you weren't meant to have sold those things in the first place. Do I make myself crystal clear?'

'Yes, Mom,' the twins said.

'Good!' She turned to me and gave me a stern look. 'I don't want to see you within ten feet of the boys for the rest of the day,' she said. 'I don't want any private acts of vengeance, got me?'

I nodded, trying to think up some way of punching the idiots out without getting to within ten feet of them. A boxing glove on the end of a pole, maybe?

'Excellent!' Mom straightened her jacket. 'OK, let's go make some money!' she said.

Denny and Bob gave me the most hate-filled looks you could imagine.

'We're gonna get you!' Denny mouthed at me the moment Mom turned away.

'Yeah, yeah, yeah!' I mouthed back. I gave them a final devastating look and I marched out of the house.

War had been declared!

There was plenty of work to do after the Yard Sale closed up. All the stuff that hadn't been sold needed to be put back into the garage and we needed to clear up the front yard so it didn't look like quite so much as if a rock festival had just left town.

Then Stacy, Pippa, Fern and I went out into the back yard to catch some late sunshine and to collaborate on listing all the stuff that had disappeared from my blue storage box. Well, that was the plan, but having Lucky with us meant we spent a lot of time chasing around in the back yard, throwing sticks and balls and crazy frantic stuff like that.

'We should tire him out,' Pippa suggested. 'Then we can get down to writing Cindy's list.'

'Good *luck*!' Fern said. 'It won't be Lucky who gets tired first, I can tell you that.'

She was right. That pup had more energy than the four of us put together. In the end Stacy came up with a great plan. We set up the bat-ball pole in the middle of the grass and Lucky played a game of whack-the-ball all on his own – running round and round the pole and bopping the ball with his snout so it went spinning around on the end of its elastic cord.

The only problem was when he managed to get the ball in his mouth. He'd run towards Fern to show her how smart he was, and as he got further away from the pole, the elastic would stretch until – *boing!* – the ball would go whipping out of his mouth and he'd arrive at Fern's feet without the ball and without any idea of where the ball had gone.

'Go fetch!' Fern would say, heartlessly, and Lucky would go bounding back to fetch the ball, his ears flopping and his tongue hanging out. And exactly the same thing would happen all over again.

'That is one dumb pooch,' Pippa said, shaking her head. 'When's he going to figure that he can't get all the way over here with that ball?'

'Never!' Fern shrieked, rolling about with laughter.

'Shall we work on my list?' I said.

'Good idea,' Stacy said.

We ended up making *two* lists.

List number one was the list of stuff that was missing from my box.

List number two was a long list of Dire and Dreadful Punishments which we thought the twins deserved.

Pippa was in charge of the pen and paper because she has the neatest writing. The thing with me and writing is that the words are totally neat inside my head, but something goes all screwy while the words are travelling down my arm and into the pen – so that by the time they hit the paper, they're kind of a mess.

'OK,' Pippa said, consulting list two. 'Here's the plan: we lure the twins down to the basement with a trail of cookies.'

'Poisoned cookies,' Fern said. 'To make them feel really awful on the way, which they totally deserve.'

'Correct,' Pippa agreed. 'Then we slam the door on them and nail it shut and leave them down there for a week.'

'A month would be better,' I suggested.

'No, a week is enough,' Pippa said. 'We don't want them to die down there.'

'Not *quickly*, anyhow,' Fern said.

'Exactly!' Pippa said. 'We leave them down there for a week on bread and water.'

'Mouldy bread and stagnant water,' Stacy said.

'Excellent!' Pippa wrote "Stagnant water".

'And we force them to eat bugs and fungus and stuff like that to survive,' Fern said.

'And we should take the light bulb out so they can't see,' I added. 'And we should let loose a whole family of hungry rats down there. And cockroaches. Great huge cockroaches. Cockroaches as big as skateboards!'

'And then, after a week, we open the door and tell them they've been forgiven, and then we tell them to come up for milk and cookies and a special showing of Splaarg the Mutant –' Pippa began.

'Space Mutant,' I corrected her.

'I beg your pardon,' Pippa said. 'A special showing of a Splaarg the Space Mutant Feature-Length TV Movie.'

'Yeah!' Fern said. 'And just as they hit the top step, we slam the door in their faces! Ha! Brilliant!'

'And we leave them down there with the stale bread and the stagnant water and the roaches and the rats for another week,' I said, rubbing my hands together. 'And then we start to get really *mean*!'

Dad came out. 'It's getting a little late, girls,' he said. 'Anyone want a lift home before your parents start thinking we sold you along with all the other stuff?'

Everyone said, 'Yes, please,' to the offer of a

lift home and we followed Dad back into the house.

Mom and Dad had counted the takings. I was really stunned by how much we had made. I guess Great-Aunt Mattie's stuff helped a whole lot. (Oh, just in case you think my mom and dad sold all Great-Aunt Mattie's stuff without telling the rest of the family, that's not true at all. The things we sold were things that no one else in the family wanted.)

Pippa and Stacy and Fern were given their share of the profits. I went along with them when my dad drove them home, and we spent the trip planning spending-sprees. Lucky was finally worn out and he sprawled across Fern and Pippa's laps and snored all the way to Fern's house.

I had enough money to buy my red shoes. Stacy had her eye on a big illustrated book about the wildlife of Yosemite Park. Fern planned on buying Lucky a new collar and a few dog toys. Pippa told us that she'd decided to put her money into her savings account.

'*Boring!*' we all yelled at her.

'OK, OK,' she said. 'I'll blow some of it on a gigantic tub of cookies'n'cream ice cream! How's that?'

'Better!' Fern said. 'Much better!'

'Well, that's our spending all figured out,' I

said. 'Tomorrow we can all get together and make plans for our sleepover party next Saturday night.'

'Excellently excellent!' Stacy said. 'And what makes the whole thing even more excellently excellent is that the new series of *Creepshow* begins next Saturday. We can all watch it together!'

Creepshow is a really spooky TV series. It was everyone's favourite last season, and we've all been looking forward to the start of the new series. If it's anything near as good as last season, I'm going to have to wear a hat to stop all my hair standing up on end. It's *that* good!

'And after we've watched *Creepshow*,' Stacy said, 'we can tell each other spooky stories with the lights out.'

'Great!' Fern said. 'I know some really grisly ones.'

'We can turn it into a total horror night!' Pippa said. 'Like a kind of early Halloween.'

I felt a shiver go down my spine even *thinking* about it. I love spooky stories – but they scare me to a total mush!

We dropped Stacy off last and then Dad drove home via the drive-through pizza parlour where we bought *two* mega-supreme-family-sized pizzas with everything on.

The boys were up in their room in disgrace

because of selling off my private personal stuff, but Mom took some pizza up to them. (Mom's just too soft on those guys! I wouldn't have given them any pizza! I wouldn't even have given them the yucky dry crusty bits from around the edges. I would have stood outside their room with slices of pizza on a plate and let the *smell* of the pizza waft in under their door to drive them crazy!)

Well, after a frantic day like that, and after two *big* slices of pizza, it was all I could do to drag myself to the bathroom to brush my teeth and then drag myself along to my room and drag myself out of my clothes and into my PJs.

You know, sometimes I feel quite envious of old people who only have to put their teeth in a glass of water to get them clean – after a long, hard day like I'd just had, I could really have done without all that up-and-down into-all-the-crevices brush-for-at-least-two-minutes stuff.

I was *pooped*. I was very pooped indeed. In fact, on the Cindy Spiegel Poopometer Scale, I was mega-pooped to the max! And that is deeply pooped, I can tell you.

I got into bed.

I stretched out.

'Ahhhhhhh!'

Erk!

'What the . . . ? *Yuuurgh!*'

What the heck was I *lying* in?

One millionth of a second later I was out of that bed like I had springs attached to my rear end. I ripped the sheets back.

Right in the middle of my bed was a big slithery splatty squidgy squoogy squodgy blob of Splaarg the Space Mutant Space Slime.

The evil twins had struck again!

That did it – I *flew* into their room in a total rage. I yelled at them that I was going to make them sorry they had ever been born.

They just laughed at me, the wretches. I had to leave before I *murdered* them then and there.

By the time I'd finished with them, they sure wouldn't be laughing. And that was a promise!

5

First thing the following morning I heard the following from the kitchen as I was going down to breakfast:

'Celia – have you seen my hat?' That was my dad talking to my mom.

'What hat?' That was Mom.

I heard, 'Blakk-blakkk-sploot-fnukk-fnukk-blakowwww!' from the living room. It sounded like the twins had their Splaarg video on in there.

'You know what hat!' Dad said. 'My *favourite* hat.'

'What about it?'

'Have you seen it?'

'Yes. Yes, I have.'

'Where is it?'

'I have no idea.'

'You just said you've seen it.'

'I have. Too often, Frank. Far too often!'

I went into the kitchen. Mom was sitting on the back step with the door open. She was typing stuff into her laptop. Dad was sitting at the table, spooning breakfast cereal around in a mournful way and sighing.

'Hi!' I said.

Dad looked at me. 'I guess you haven't seen my hat either, have you, honey? My lucky green hat.'

'Not since yesterday,' I said. 'You were wearing it all day.'

Dad nodded sadly. 'That's right. And now it's gone! Vanished!' He shook his head. 'I can't understand it!'

Mom had her back to us but I could see her shoulders going up and down, which strongly suggested to me that she was trying real hard not to burst out laughing.

'Maybe the hat angels came for it overnight,' she said. 'Maybe it's gone to hat heaven.'

'I'm sure I put it down on the desk in the office,' Dad said in a baffled voice. (For 'office' read 'small back room'.) 'But this morning when I went to get it, it was gone! And I really need some luck – I still haven't heard from the competition people and the weekend break is next week!' He looked across to my mom. 'Celia? I'm beginning to think maybe I haven't won. What do you think?'

She turned and looked at him. 'Do you want honest or toned-down?'

He sighed. 'Toned-down.'

'You haven't won,' Mom said. 'Not in a million years have you won. You never win *anything*, Frank.'

'But I've been wearing my lucky hat!' Dad said miserably. 'Except that now the darned thing has vanished!'

I guess I should explain about Dad's lucky hat. Dad likes to go fishing with his pals. Three years ago, he borrowed the floppy green wreck of a hat from one of his friends, and he caught the biggest fish he had ever caught in his entire life! It was such a big fish that he didn't even need to fake how big it was like he usually does. Dad decided he caught the monster fish because of the influence of the hat, so he bought the hat off his friend and he's been wearing it 'for luck' ever since. Except for the times when my mom has hidden it or tried to throw it away.

And the competition? Well, Dad likes to enter the kind of competitions that you find on the back of cereal boxes and in the back pages of our local newspaper. But like Mom said: he never wins! That still doesn't stop him, though.

The latest competition was to win a weekend away for two up on the shores of Lake Michigan. I don't remember what Dad had to do to win – he enters so many competitions I kind of lose track, you know?

I had a pretty good idea of what had happened to Dad's lucky hat. It was probably in itsy-bitsy pieces at the far end of the waste disposal! Not that Mom was going to let on.

Just then, Denny came racing in and dived into the fridge.

'Hey, Denny,' Dad asked. 'Have you seen my lucky hat?'

'Sure,' came Denny's voice from inside the fridge. 'Mom had it earlier this morning. I saw her walking in the backyard with it.'

'You saw no such thing!' Mom said.

Aha! I thought. The compost heap!

Denny's face appeared around the fridge door. 'Sure I did,' he said, ignoring the look on Mom's face. 'I saw you out of our bedroom window. You had it in your hand. I saw you.'

Dad gave Mom a withering look. He got up and stepped past her to go and retrieve his beloved lucky hat from the compost heap.

'Mom? Is there any chocolate ice cream?' Denny said.

'There is. But you're not getting any,' Mom said crossly. 'You and your brother should be out trying to get Cindy's things back, not sitting in front of the television guzzling ice cream – especially at this hour!'

'We were going to do it later,' Denny said.

'You're going to do it right now, young man,' Mom said, getting up.

'But we're watching a video,' Denny protested.

'You can watch it later.'

Still whining and complaining, Denny was herded out of the kitchen. That served him right for giving the game away about Dad's hat!

I just hoped they'd be able to track down my things.

Whether they got all my stuff back or not, the terrible twins were in for a lot of foot-slogging around the neighbourhood that day – and they deserved it!

'Mom, could I have a serious word with you, please?' I asked. Mom was in the 'office' bashing away at her computer. The screen was full of really dull-looking spreadsheets and grisly stuff like that.

'Yes, honey,' she said, still typing.

'Good.' I perched on the two-drawer filing cabinet and waited for her to pay me some attention.

'Mom, could I have a really, really serious word with you about something totally and utterly important?' I said.

'I told you yes, honey,' Mom said, tap-tap-tapping away.

'Ahem!'

'Go right ahead, honey, I'm listening.'

'I want to dye my hair bright green,' I said. 'I want a tongue stud and I want you to buy me a motorbike for my next birthday so I can drive cross-country with a punk rock band that I just met. Is that OK?'

Mom stopped typing. She swivelled around in her chair and looked at me. 'Message received and understood,' she said with a smile. 'You have my full attention, Cindy. What's the problem?'

'Denny and Bob are the problem,' I said. 'They're going to ruin my sleepover. I just *know* they are.'

'Look, I know how you feel sometimes, honey,' Mom said. 'They drive us all wild at one time or another. But I've already told you: no way can we take them way out of town and just abandon them in the woods.' She chuckled. 'It's not *legal*, honey.'

I clasped my hands in my lap. 'Mom,' I said sternly. 'This *is* actually rather serious, if that's OK with you.'

'Sorry,' Mom said. 'Go right ahead.'

'Do you remember the last sleepover party we had?'

'Vividly,' Mom said with a shudder. 'There were about a dozen of you, and you didn't shut up until about half-past five in the morning.'

'There were only ten of us, actually, but what I was thinking of was –'

'And the next morning you were all rushing around the house like a bunch of hysterical hyperactive sleep-deprived monkeys,' Mom continued.

'Mom! Stop exaggerating!'

'And I wound up with two garbage bags full of debris and leftovers from all the food you consumed. And some of the stains are still on the living room carpet from that competition you set up where you had to invent the most disgusting sandwich *ever*.'

'Yeah, well,' I said. 'That was Fern's idea, not mine, but the point I'm trying to make is –'

'And Denise was sick all up the stair carpet.'

'No, she wasn't,' I said. 'That was Paula – and she *nearly* made it to the bathroom,' I added. 'And, besides, we all told her not to try eating that sandwich she'd made.' (By the way, it was an instant coffee granules, mustard and chilli sauce sandwich.)

'And Pippa blew up the hi-fi.'

'She didn't blow it up,' I said. 'There was just a bit of smoke, that's all. And once Dad got all the melted chocolate out of the CD player, it worked just fine!'

'And you had running battles through the house with your brothers all night,' Mom said.

'*Exactly!*' I hollered. 'That's *exactly* what I was thinking of.' I gave Mom my most serious look. 'Mom, I want very deeply and sincerely to help in any way I can to make this sleepover party the most quiet and reasonable and responsible sleepover party *ever*. Are you with me on this?'

'I most certainly am,' Mom said. 'What did you have in mind? Sleeping pills in your milk-shakes to knock you all out for the night?'

I held up my forefingers. 'I don't really think that will be necessary,' I said. 'But I do have a plan which I think you may find of interest.'

'I'm all ears,' Mom said.

'My suggestion is this,' I said. 'How about you arrange for Denny and Bob to spend the night with Grammy?'

'Great idea.'

'Now, before you totally dismiss this thought, I'd like for you to consider that most of the disruption at the last sleepover was caused by . . . uh . . . *sorry*?' I stared at her. 'What did you just say?'

Mom grinned. 'I said that I thought it was a great idea. I'll arrange it with Grammy. No problem.'

'Oh!'

Mom laughed. 'What's wrong, honey? Can't you take yes for an answer?'

'I had a whole batch of reasons why you should send the twins over to Grammy's,' I said. 'I didn't get a chance to tell you any of them.'

'I can change my mind, if that suits you better,' Mom said.

'No way!' I jumped off the filing cabinet and gave her a quick hug. 'You're the best mom in the whole world, do you know that?'

'Yes,' Mom said. 'Yes, I do.'

That afternoon the gang met up (Pippa calls it 'convened' – she would!) at Stacy's house to discuss the details of our sleepover get-together.

Everyone was really pleased that Mom had agreed to pack the terrible twins off to Grammy's for the night. If there was one thing guaranteed to wreck any plans we might make for a bumper-super sleepover, it would be having to share the house with Denny and Bob. Especially as they were at war with me right then.

First item on the agenda (Stacy insisted on a written agenda) was who we should invite. Fern was all for a humungous great party with twenty-five people or more.

'Where will they all sleep, Fern?' I asked. 'Hanging up in a closet?'

'And how could twenty-five people all fit into Cindy's living room to watch *Creepshow*?' Pippa added.

'Mom would never go for it,' I said. 'Not never, ever. Not after last time. Not even with Denny and Bob out of the house.'

'I think it would be more fun if it was just the four of us,' Stacy suggested. 'That way everyone gets a seat on the couch to watch TV, and there's plenty of room for us all to sleep in Cindy's room.'

'Good point,' I said. 'Remember the last sleepover we had?' As I had just reminded Mom, there were ten of us. We had to sleep on the floor in the living room. Denny and Bob spent the whole night pestering us and being a total pain. Mom was up and down the stairs about a million times trying to keep things under control.

'I don't know why these things are called *sleep*overs!' Mom said afterwards. 'They should be called *wide-awake-overs*. I hardly slept a wink all night!'

Moms have no idea! I mean, what's the point of having friends over for the night if all you do is *go to sleep*? Besides which, most of the noise was caused by us fighting off midnight attacks by the twins.

Anyway, we talked things over for a while longer and Fern kept right on insisting we should invite the whole neighbourhood and have what she called a 'Mega-Scare-in Freakadelic Horrorfest'!

Pippa said we should have a secret vote and decide the whole thing democratically. So Stacy tore four sheets out of her notebook and each of us secretly wrote the number of people we thought should be invited to the sleepover.

We handed the folded sheets of paper over to Pippa.

The result was: Three votes for just the four of us.

One vote for 20,000 people at the very least, including Count Dracula the big boss Vampire and any alien space-people who happen to be in the neighbourhood at the time.

Yeah, and guess who voted which way!

Well, we spent most of the rest of the afternoon making up lists of stuff we'd like to eat and drink (very important!) and making another list of what videos we wanted to rent. *Creepshow* is only an hour long, so we needed some more stuff for the rest of the night.

Fern said she'd take a look at the stock in her

folks' store and see if there was anything good that she could borrow for the night.

'Something scary,' Stacy said. 'Remember, the theme for the sleepover is *ultra-super-scariness*!'

'I think there are some horror movies in stock,' Fern said. 'I'll check it out.'

'Get the grisliest and gruesomest ones,' Pippa said. 'Lots of blood and gore and people's guts hanging out and eyes being pecked out by crows and skeletons coming up out of graves, and –'

'Pippa!' I said. 'Hel-*lo*! Like, my mom is totally not going to allow us to watch movies full of blood and gore and crows pecking people's eyeballs out! No way!'

Pippa sighed. 'Excuse me for being blunt, Cindy, but sometimes your mom is no *fun* at all,' she said.

'Does your mom let *you* watch movies like that?' Fern asked Pippa.

'I'm sure she would if I asked,' Pippa said.

'So,' Fern said, 'if I can get a major-league gruesome adult horror movie on video, and if Cindy's mom won't let us watch it at her house – we can all go to your house to watch it, right?'

Pippa blinked at her. 'Can we get back to deciding what we want to eat next Saturday?'

she said very quickly. I guess she didn't want to have her theory tested!

By the time we'd finished listing all the stuff we wanted to snack-out on at the sleepover, we really would have been able to feed 20,000 people. But like Stacy said, you can never ever have *too much* nice stuff to eat. And even if you're so stuffed that you're going cross-eyed, you can always find room for ice-cream.

As I was cycling home, I saw Andy Melniker sitting on a wall playing with a yo-yo. Andy Melniker is in our form at school. He's a little weird at times, but I get on OK with him, so I stopped to say hi.

'Hi!' I said.

'Hi!' he said back.

'Neat yo-yo,' I said. It had a swirly fluorescent green pattern on it. It made my eyes go wibbly-wobbly when it spun. Andy was pretty good at yo-yoing it up and down.

'It's called the Green Goblin,' Andy said.

'Can I try?' I asked.

Andy handed it over. The yo-yo yo-yoed down to the end of its string and just sat there. I did my best to get it moving, but nothing worked.

'I guess it's a knack,' I said, handing it back.

'I guess so,' Andy said, spinning the yo-yo every which way like it was the easiest thing in the world. 'I saw your brothers in the ice-cream parlour in the mall a while back.'

'When was this?' I asked. What the heck were they doing in the mall? They were meant to be out hunting down my stuff.

'They were there around noon when I went in with my folks,' Andy said, yo-yoing up and down and around and around and to and fro like he wasn't even thinking about it. 'And they were still there around three o'clock when we left.'

'Wha-at!'

I didn't wait to watch Andy perform any more yo-yo tricks.

I cycled home like a bullet.

I went running into the house to tell Mom. I heard voices coming from the living room.

'Are you telling me you weren't able to find a single one of Cindy's things?' Mom was saying.

'We tried and tried,' Denny whined. 'We've been out looking all day! We've been to hundreds of people's houses. Hundreds and hundreds! It's not our fault we can't remember who bought the stuff.'

'We did our best,' Bob added. 'Honest we did!'

Honest! I'd give them *honest*!

I stormed into the living room. 'If you spent

all day searching for my things how come Andy Melniker saw you stuffing your faces with ice-cream at the mall?' I demanded angrily.

'We were only in there for two minutes,' Bob said. He gave Mom his ultra-innocent look. 'We couldn't go all day with nothin' to eat.'

Bob nodded. 'That's right. We ate it super-fast and went straight back out again.'

I slammed my fists down on my hips. 'Oh, *really*?' I said. 'So how come Andy just told me he saw you in there at twelve o'clock when he arrived, and that you were still in there at three o'clock when he left?'

Bob's mouth opened but he couldn't think of anything to say.

'We . . . we went back again,' Denny said, obviously thinking fast. 'Yes, that's right, now I think about it. We went in there at twelve o'clock, and then we went back there again at three o'clock.' He looked at Bob. '*Remember*?'

'Duh . . . der . . . dohhh . . .' Bob mumbled, looking about as dumb as the first-prize winner of the Dumbest Mule at a Dumb Mule Convention. 'Uh . . . oh . . . yeah!' He gave Mom a hopeful smile. 'That's what we did. What Denny said! I remember now!'

Mom looked at them. Whoo! I knew that look, all right. Were they ever in big trouble!

'You two are *so* grounded!' she said. 'And

you are going to hand over your share of the Yard Sale profits to your sister, to make up for losing her things.'

Well! That just about settled their hash! They'd asked for it – and Mom was dishing it out in spades.

As they slunk upstairs, they looked so miserable that I could almost feel sorry for them.

I did say *almost*.

6

I was expecting some major fall-out from my brothers, I can tell you. But it was all strangely quiet for the rest of the day. Like the quiet part of a disaster movie just before the hurricane hits, or the volcano blows, or the ship hits an iceberg.

I examined my bed really thoroughly before I got into it. No green Splaarg splats. No rubber snakes or lizards. No spiders.

Strange.

I couldn't believe the boys were going to just let it ride. They had to be planning something. But what? One thing was for sure, I had to be on my guard, like, twenty-four hours a day.

I lay in bed that night listening for any sounds outside my door. I tried to keep myself awake and vigilant, but I kept dozing off.

And then I heard a creak – right outside my door. Aha! The long-awaited attack was coming at last! Well, I'd see about that!

I slipped out of bed. I grabbed a pillow and

tip-toed over to the door.

Yeah! There was definitely someone outside.

So, they figured they would come steaming in with water-pistols or whatever and catch me asleep, huh? No way!

I climbed onto a chair I'd put behind the door. I lifted the pillow over my head. They wouldn't know what hit them!

The door opened.

Three! Two! One! Whackaroonie! Down came the pillow with plenty of beef behind it. I was going to get them but good!

'What the – owww!' I got someone all right – I got Mom!

'Cindy!' She stared at me kind of woozily.

'Oh, sorry, Mom,' I said. 'I thought you were someone else.'

She gave me one of her special looks. (I'm not a real big fan of my mom's *special* looks.)

'Bed!' she said. 'Right now!'

She tucked me in. 'And, Cindy? No more lying in wait for your brothers. Leave the discipline to me, please. I don't want this to turn into World War Three.'

'Yes, Mom,' I said. 'Sorry, about your head, Mom,' I added. I gave her a hopeful grin. 'Good thing it was only a pillow. Good thing it wasn't a chair, huh?'

'Hmmm,' she said.

Heck!

The main topic of conversation in Homeroom on Monday morning was the new *Creepshow* series that was kicking off next Saturday night. The TV people had been running trailers for about a month and everyone was really looking forward to it. Some of the scenes in the trailers looked really good.

Like, there was one scene where an oil-paint portrait of a guy hanging on a wall in an old house suddenly came alive just as someone was walking past. The painted guy's arm reached down out of the picture frame and the innocent passer-by was grabbed by the collar and yanked up into the picture.

The really creepy thing was that the face in the painting changed into the face of the guy who had just been snatched. And he'd be trapped in limbo in the weird painting until he could grab another person and drag them into the painting to take his place . . . for all eternity!

And that was just *one* episode.

Of course, big-mouth Sophie Carpenter had plenty to say on the subject. She always does. 'I don't know why you guys are getting so excited about a dumb TV show, when we have a genuine, real-life haunted house in our very own neighbourhood.'

'If you mean *your* house, we already know about it,' Fern said. 'The house of the living-dead-head!'

'Well, har-har,' Sophie said. 'Seen any good *aliens* lately, Fern?' (I guess I ought to mention that Fern has a little quirk: she believes that aliens disguised as human beings live in our town. I guess a person is entitled to have the odd way-out idea; after all, Sophie does: she thinks she's a really *interesting* person.)

'So, where's this haunted house?' Stacy asked.

'On the corner of Fairview and Halifax,' Sophie said.

'I know the one you mean,' Peter Bolger said. 'It's a big old place – all falling to bits. No one lives there. It's all boarded up and everything.'

'That's exactly the place,' Sophie said mysteriously. 'And you're absolutely right, Peter – no one *lives* there. Not now. Not any more.' She looked around at us. 'But that doesn't mean the place is *empty*.'

A shiver ran down my spine. I knew Sophie was deliberately trying to spook us, but the problem is that I spook really easily.

'So, who's haunting the house?' Stacy asked. 'The ghost of Big Fibs Past, or what?'

'The ghost of a crazy old woman who died in there years and years ago,' Sophie said. 'My mom told me all about her. Her name was Joan Ugg.'

'Joan *Ugg*?' Pippa said.

'Yes, Joan Ugg. That's Ugg with two Gs,' Sophie said. 'She used to be a real famous writer of spooky books for kids. A long time ago. But then publishers stopped wanting to publish her books because they were getting too weird.'

'What kind of weird?' Fern asked.

'*Seriously* weird,' Sophie said. 'Stories about murdering kids and chopping them up into weenie little pieces and putting them into pies and selling the pies to school cafeterias. It's totally the truth.'

'So, what happened to her?' Pippa asked.

'She went insane,' Sophie said with relish. 'My mom said she received one too many rejection letters for her books, and one day she just blocked up all the doors and windows from the inside and just sat there in the dark in her old rocking chair – rocking to and fro and not eating or drinking – until she was as thin as a skeleton –' Sophie's eyes were like saucers. 'And she just sat there like that until she starved to death!'

'How comes your mom knows all about this

when no one else in the world has ever heard of it?' Larry Franco asked.

'Because my mom is best friends with the wife of the police officer who was the first guy to break into the house after the neighbours complained about the smell,' Sophie said.

'Ewww!' a lot of us said when she mentioned the smell.

Sophie nodded. 'Yeah, the place totally reeked, and, like, old Miss Ugg had been half-eaten by rats and stuff. According to the wife of the police officer who bust the door down, she was, like, a total gruesome, grisly, ghastly *mess*. She'd been sitting there dead for over a month when they found her.'

'How were her eyes?' Pippa asked.

Sophie stared at her. 'Huh?'

'Had her eyes been pecked out by crows or eaten by rats?' Pippa asked.

'*Pippa!*' I screeched. Talk about an awful thing to want to know.

'I was interested is all,' Pippa shrugged.

'I don't know what happened to her eyes,' Sophie said with a shudder. 'But I do know that the ghost of old Joan Ugg still haunts the house, and that's a stone fact!'

'Says who?' asked Fern.

'Says anyone who's been anywhere near the place,' Sophie said. 'If you listen at the door you can hear a creaking noise from way inside the house. *Creak, creak, creak.* That's the ghost of Joan Ugg rocking in her rocking chair. And if you're crazy enough to go into the house, the ghost will get you and drag you down to the cellar – which is where she keeps the butcher knives and the big mincing machine – and once you're down there, you'll never see the light of day again. You'll be totally murdered! And then you'll be put into pies and sold to a school, and kids will eat you for lunch!'

I felt a little faint. I'd sure never look at our cafeteria burgers the same way again! Gruuugh! I mean: imagine *eating* someone like Peter Bolger – his nose is always running! Ewwww!

'Yeah, sure!' Stacy said. 'I really believe you, Sophie.'

'It's true!' Sophie said.

'Well, for one,' Stacy said, 'I don't believe there are any such things as ghosts – and for two, I wouldn't be scared of them, even if they did exist! And for three, I don't believe a single solitary word of any of what you just said. I've never heard of a children's writer called Joan Ugg. Tell me the name of one of her books, if she was so famous.'

'Her books went out of print years and years ago,' Sophie insisted. 'I don't know the names of any of them.' Her eyes narrowed. 'But if you're so sure there's no such thing as ghosts, why don't you go into Joan Ugg's house and *prove* it?'

'Sure!' Stacy said. 'No problem! Any time!'

'I'll come with you,' Fern said. 'I'll bring my camera. I'd like to take a picture of a ghost.'

'One look at the house and you'll run like scared little rabbits,' Sophie said.

'Says you!' Fern declared.

'Yeah! Says me!' Sophie retorted. 'Put your money where your mouth is, Stacy. I totally *double-dare* you to go into Joan Ugg's house!'

'Done!' Stacy said.

'How are you going to prove you really went in there?' Peter Bolger asked. 'You have to be able to prove it!'

'I'll take a picture of the rocking chair,' Fern said. She grinned. 'And if there's a ghost sitting in it, I'll ask her to say cheese, and I'll take a picture of her, too! How's that for proof!'

'Yeah, and I'll go, too,' Pippa said. 'I'm not afraid of any ghost.'

Stacy looked at me.

I blinked at her.

Everyone else turned and looked at me.

'What?' I croaked. For some reason my mouth had gone really dry.

'I'm going to check out this so-called

61

haunted house,' Stacy said. 'And Fern's coming, and Pippa's coming, too.' She looked at me kind of like she expected me to say something.

I could see the terrible old haunted house really clearly in my mind. I could see the rocking chair. I could hear it creaking away in there. *Creak, creak creak*. And I could just about see the ghost of old Joan Ugg dragging me down to her Cellar of Evil to mince me up into meatloaf or Cindy-burgers! Ulp!

'She's scared!' Betsy-Jane Garside crowed. 'Cindy's a scaredy-cat!' (Oooh! I just hate that girl!)

'I am not!' I said.

'Are, too!'

'Am not!'

'Prove it!'

'I darned well will!' I said fiercely. 'There's nothing I like better than a fun bit of ghost-hunting. And for your information, Betsy-Jane, I plan on being the first person in the so-called haunted house, and if I meet up with the ghost of Joan Ugg, I'm going to say "how do you do" to her and shake her hand. So there!'

'Excellent!' Stacy said. 'Excellently excellent! We'll *all* go over there together!'

'Tonight!' Sophie said.

'I can't, tonight,' I squeaked. 'I have to help my mom tonight. I promised.'

'Tomorrow, then!' Sophie gave me a hard look. 'Or are you a big chicken who's trying to weasel out of it, Cindy?'

'Chickens don't *weasel*,' Pippa said.

'I'm no chicken,' I said. 'Tomorrow night is just fine and dandy by me!'

'We can't go there at night,' Pippa pointed out. 'Our folks won't let us out at night. Especially not if we have to tell 'em we're planning on dropping in on the ghost of a crazy old school-kid-mincer type of a person.'

'Tomorrow afternoon after school, then,' Stacy said.

'Done!' Sophie said with a big grin. 'And you come back with pictures of the old rocking chair to prove it, right?'

'Right!' Fern said determinedly.

'Right!' Stacy said firmly.

'Right!' Pippa said grimly.

There was a pause. Everyone looked at me again.

'Right,' I squeaked weakly.

I have a confession to make. Don't laugh, but I am totally scared to little tiny pieces of ghosts.

7

'I have a confession to make, guys,' I told my pals. It was the afternoon of the same day. We were in my room with strawberry milkshakes and various packs of nibbles supplied by my mom. 'I don't want to seem like a total wet weed and a feeble little worm-kind-of-thing,' I said, 'but I'm not totally . . . uh . . .' I gave them an anxious look. 'Look, guys, do we really have to go over to that haunted house-place tomorrow afternoon? I mean, is there some way we could get out of it?'

'Are you trying to tell us that you're scared of ghosts?' Fern said, staring at me.

'No way,' I said. 'What do you think I am, some kind of big baby?'

They all looked at me.

'OK! OK! I'm scared of ghosts!' I squeaked. 'What if Sophie was telling the truth? What if we go in there and crazy old Joan Ugg really is still sitting there in her rocking chair – *dead*! And what if she grabs us and drags us down to the cellar and chops us up and puts us into pies and stuff? I don't want to be murdered and chopped up and put in a pie. It's not *nice*!'

'Chill out, Cindy,' Fern said. 'You're babbling. Get a grip!'

'Calm down,' Stacy said. 'Ghosts don't exist, Cindy. Tell her, Pippa. Tell her that ghosts don't exist.'

Pippa looked at me. 'Ghosts don't exist,' she said. '. . . probably!'

Stacy frowned at her. 'Pippa!'

Pippa shrugged. 'Just because science has been unable to prove definitively that ghosts *do* exist, that doesn't mean they absolutely *don't* exist.'

'That does it!' I said. 'No way am I going within twenty million trillion miles of Joan Ugg's house. I knew it! I just knew it! It's totally haunted.' I got up and headed for my closet. (This is kind of embarrassing, but when I get spooked, I feel a whole lot safer if I can sit in the bottom of my closet.)

Stacy jumped up and barred my way. 'Do you trust me, Cindy?' she asked.

'Sure,' I said, surprised.

'So, trust me when I tell you there are no such things as ghosts,' she said. 'There are absolutely without a shadow of a doubt no such things as ghosts.'

I looked at her.

'But Sophie said –'

'Sophie Carpenter should be forced to go around with a T-shirt with *I Am A Big Liar* written on it,' Fern said. 'Sophie wouldn't know the truth if it poked her in the eye.'

'But Pippa said –'

Stacy looked at Pippa. 'Tell her ghosts don't exist,' she said. 'If you don't tell her that ghosts don't exist, she won't come to the house with us tomorrow afternoon and everyone will think she's a total cowardy custard.'

Pippa looked at me. 'If Sophie Carpenter says there's a ghost in the house on the corner of Fairview and Halifax,' she said slowly, 'then that's a really good reason for believing there *isn't* a ghost in the house on the corner of Fairview and Halifax.' She nodded. 'That's my opinion, anyhow.'

I thought about this. Pippa was right about one thing: Sophie was always making up stories to try and impress people.

Stacy looked at me. 'Well?' she said.

I grinned. 'I'm not scared of Sophie Carpenter's dumb stories!' I said determinedly. 'I'm coming! Definitely!'

'Way to go, Cindy!' Fern said with a big grin. 'And if there are any ghosts in there, we'll keep 'em off you.'

'I think we should celebrate this agreement,' Pippa said. 'More milkshakes!'

'Four more milkshakes coming right up,' I said. I yanked the door open.

Denny came tumbling into the room and went splat on the carpet.

We all stared at him in amazement.

'Someone's been eavesdropping!' Stacy said.

Denny staggered up. I grabbed him before he could make a run for it.

'I wasn't eavesdropping!' he squealed. 'I was tying my shoelace.'

We looked down at his feet. He was in his socks.

'I . . . I mean, I dropped a dime,' he stammered, pointing at the floor just outside my door. 'I dropped a dime and . . . uh . . . I was . . . looking for it.'

Stacy stepped out into the hallway. 'I don't see any coin,' she said.

'It must have rolled away,' Denny explained.

'It couldn't have rolled far,' I said. 'Not on such a thick carpet. Anyhow, what were you doing up this end of the hall, Denny?' My room is the last one along the hallway. Denny and Bob's room is right at the back of the house.

'I was going to the bathroom, for your

information,' Denny said. 'Like, I really have to report to *you*!'

I hauled him out into the hallway. 'The bathroom is that way!' I said, pointing to the bathroom door. 'You walked straight past it.'

'The quarter rolled this way,' Denny said. 'I came to get it.'

'It was a dime a second ago,' Pippa said.

'I meant a dime,' Denny said. 'It fell out of my pocket and rolled over here. Not that it's any of your business!'

'It certainly is my business if some sneaky little toad is caught outside my bedroom door, listening to my private conversations,' I growled.

'I wasn't listening to your dumb private conversations,' Denny said. 'Like, I'm totally interested in some dumb ghost story!'

'If you weren't listening, how come you know we were talking about ghosts?' I snarled.

'I didn't,' he said. 'I don't know what you were talking about. You could have been talking about anything. How should I know? I wasn't listening.'

'So, you just *guessed* we were talking about ghosts, is that it?' Stacy said.

'Yes. No.' He blinked up at us. 'Let me go!'

He yanked away from me. I let go of him and he went sprawling on the hall carpet.

He gave me such a glare.

'While you're down there, why don't you carry on looking for your dime?' I said. I stepped over him.

'Owww!'

'Oh, so sorry, Denny. Was that your ear I just kicked? Total accident!' I headed downstairs. 'Four chocolate milkshakes coming up, guys!' I said.

Denny slunk back to his room, scowling at me and rubbing his sore ear. Well, let's face it, people who press the sides of their heads up against other people's doors are going to get sore ears – it stands to reason.

It was a nice sunny afternoon. The four of us stood at the corner of Fairview and Halifax with our bikes. Fern had her camera slung around her neck. It was one of those cameras that deliver instant pictures. You press a button and – whoosh – the finished picture pops out through a slot in the front.

The house was a really old clapboard building, set way back off the road in a totally neglected patch of grass and overgrown bushes. It didn't look *exactly* like you'd expect a haunted house to look. But then again, it didn't look like the kind of place you'd want to throw a party, if you know what I mean.

It was pretty obvious that no one lived there. There was a for sale sign out front on a pole – but even that looked like it had been standing there for years. The ground-floor windows were boarded up and the whole place looked really miserable and abandoned.

Fern fiddled with her camera. 'I need to check the flash,' she said, peering into the lens. 'There won't be any electricity on in there, that's for sure.' She pressed the button and the flash went off in her face. 'Yowlp!' she yelled. 'Whoa! *Bright!*' She blinked in a dazzled kind of a way.

'I guess the flash is working,' Stacy said. She looked at us. 'Well? Are we going to do this or what?'

'We are,' Pippa said. She eyed the old house. 'It doesn't look so scary,' she said. She wheeled her bike across the road. I followed her. Stacy came next, towing Fern along as Fern still couldn't see a thing because of the flash having gone off right in her face.

We laid our bikes down in the long unmown grass and walked up the weedy and cracked front path.

'Uh, guys,' I said, 'what's the plan if we see something in there?'

Stacy looked at me. 'Such as what?'

'Uh . . . well . . . maybe some homeless

tramp kind of a person might have moved in there,' I suggested.

'Or rats,' Pippa said cheerfully. 'There could be rats. Whole families of rats.'

'Cool!' Fern said. 'I should have brought Lucky. I bet he'd just love to chase some nice juicy fat rats.'

'Fern!' I said. '*Please!*'

Stacy walked up the front steps.

Creak. Creak. Creak.

'They creaked!' I screeched, perfectly calmly.

'Cindy, don't panic,' Pippa said, patting me on the shoulder. 'They're old wooden steps – sure they're going to creak.'

'I'm not panicking,' I said.

Stacy walked under the veranda. She peered in through a gap in the boards that were covering one of the front windows.

'See anything?' Pippa called softly.

'Nope,' Stacy said. 'The glass is too dirty to see anything in there.'

Fern went stamping up the steps and rattled the front door. 'Darn!' she said. 'Locked!' She crouched down and flipped the mail box. 'Hey! Old lady! You in there?' She grinned around at us then yelled again. 'I'd like to take a few pictures, if that's OK! Hello! Anyone home?' She banged on the door again then shrugged. 'I guess there's no one home.'

It was kind of hard to feel totally scared to death with Fern prancing about up there, grinning and laughing and treating the whole thing like a big joke.

By then I was beginning to think it *was* just a big joke, too, to be honest. Sophie Carpenter's big joke!

'Maybe there's a way in around the back,' Pippa suggested.

I followed her up onto the veranda and we all walked around to the side of the house. It had a neglected kind of smell – like no one had cared for it in ages. Poor old house! And the paint was peeling and there was garbage lying around.

'Aha!' Stacy said.

She pointed. The boards had fallen away from one of the windows and the sash was half open. The piece of the room that we could see through the grimy glass was very dark.

'Did anyone think to bring a flashlight?' Pippa asked.

No one had.

'Well, that was really smart!' Pippa said.

'So, where's *your* flashlight, Pippa?' Fern asked.

'At home,' Pippa said. 'But at least I remembered that we'd forgotten.'

Stacy rolled her eyes. 'Amazingly helpful,

Pippa!' she said. She looked at us. 'Well, guys, what's the plan?'

'We go in, we take a few snap-shots, and we get out,' Fern said.

'Do you think it's *allowed*?' I asked. They looked at me. I spread my hands out. 'The house must belong to someone. We could get in trouble. Guys? Couldn't we? Huh? Couldn't we get in trouble if we, like, break in?'

'Hel-*lo*!' Fern said. 'The window is totally open. What's there to break?' She folded herself up and climbed in through the open window.

Stacy shrugged. 'Who's to know?' she said. 'Like Fern said: a couple of snaps and then we're out of there.'

Stacy climbed into the dark hole.

Pippa looked at me.

I looked at Pippa.

'Are you still scared that there might be ghosts?' she said.

'Who, me?' I said with a merry laugh. 'No way! Ghosts! *Pfhuh!*'

'So how come your voice is all shaky?'

'It isn't,' I said, trying my hardest to make my voice sound less shaky. 'I'm just a little concerned that we could get into bad trouble if the owners or whoever catch us sneaking around in there.'

'Not very likely,' Pippa said. She stretched

out one of her long skinny legs and stuck it through the open window. She sat on the sill. 'If you want my opinion, I still think rats are the biggest problem we're going to have in there,' she said quite happily. She smiled. 'Apparently, the best way to disable an attacking rat is to whack it across the snout with a stick just as it leaps for your throat.'

'Umm . . .' I had a few questions I needed answering about Pippa's anti-rat defence techniques, but she vanished into the house before I had a chance to say a word. I looked around for a rat-whacking stick.

There wasn't one to hand.

Maybe a karate chop would do the business?

I stood there staring at the dark hole into which my three best friends had vanished.

I had two choices. Either I could climb in through that window and be as brave as the bravest person who ever did a brave thing; or I could just hang around out here and wait for my friends to come back.

They'd understand. My best pals in the whole wide world would understand. I mean, it wasn't like anyone was going to say, *Hey, you big scaredy-cat – get in here! Or do I have to come out there and drag you in?*

It's not like *that* was going to happen.

Fern's face appeared at the open window.

'Hey, you big scaredy-cat,' she said. 'Get in here! Or do I have to come out there and drag you in?'

8

'I'm totally not scared, you know,' I explained to Fern as she yanked me in through the half-open window. 'I was just looking for a stick to whack the rats with!'

'There aren't any rats,' Fern said. 'There's *nothin*'.'

The room was pretty gloomy and it took a little while for my eyes to get used to the dark.

But once my eyes had gotten used to the dimness in there I could see that we were in a big room with bare floorboards and dingy, grubby walls. There were a few shabby pieces of dusty old furniture here and there. There were no rats. And there was certainly no ghost.

I can't honestly say I felt really *happy* to be in there, but I was beginning to think maybe we weren't all going to be dragged down to the Cellar of Evil and . . . well . . . and all the rest.

Fern marched off to the open door. 'C'mon, guys,' she said. 'Let's check the rest of this dump out.' She called into the hall. 'Hello! Hello, anyone! Miss Ugg?' She stamped off. 'Old Lady Ugg? Uggy-wuggy? Yoo-hoo? Come out, come out, wherever you are!'

'She'll totally scare the ghost off, yelling like that,' Pippa said. 'We'll never get to see it!'

I stared at her. 'Excuse me?'

She grinned. 'It's notoriously difficult to take pictures of ghosts,' she said. 'We'd be totally famous if we took some real pictures of a ghost. We'd probably get our names in the newspapers and everything. We might even get on TV.'

'But you said . . . there . . . were . . . no . . . ghookerkkerkkkle . . . gruuugh . . .' All of a sudden my hair seemed to be standing on end. The room began to dance around in the oddest way.

'Cindy?' Stacy asked. 'Are you OK?'

'Yip,' I said. 'Yip, yip.'

'Pippa? What did you say to her?'

'Nothing,' Pippa said. 'Nothing at all.'

'Except?'

'Well, except that Fern was going to frighten the ghost off, the way she's behaving.'

'Oh, great, Pippa! Now look what you've done to her!'

'I think she's hyperventilating,' Pippa said helpfully. 'Do you think it would snap her out of it if I smacked her around the chops? That always seems to do the trick in movies.'

The room stopped dancing around and I found myself blinking into Stacy and Pippa's concerned faces.

'I'm fine,' I said. 'If you hit me, Pippa, I'll bite your nose off!'

'She's fine,' Stacy said. 'Let's go see where Fern's gone, and –'

'Yo! Guys!' It was Fern, yelling at the top of her voice. 'Come see what I found! Woh, boy! In-*cred*-ible!'

She didn't sound scared – just excited. We ran out of the room. There was a big, wide hallway with several doors leading off and a staircase going up to the second floor. Fern was standing in an open doorway.

We crowded around her.

The room was pretty much like the one we'd just come from. You know – bare walls with those odd grubby marks where pictures used to hang. Bare floorboards. Old bits and pieces of furniture. A big built-in closet. Dust and dirt. And . . .

'Ohmigosh!' Stacy hissed. 'Will you take a look at that!'

Standing right in front of the big closet was an old rocking chair.

We goggled at it.

Joan Ugg's rocking chair. Oo-er!

'Guys,' I said in a really small voice. 'I think we should get out of here.'

'Why?' Fern asked.

'Be-be-because of th-th-that . . .' I said, pointing at the chair.

'It's only an old rocking chair,' Stacy said.

'But Sophie *said* about the rocking chair,' I squeaked. 'She said the ghost sat in the rocking chair. So if there really is a rocking chair – there must be a . . . gug-gog-gig-ghost!'

'Don't be silly,' Pippa said. 'My gran has a rocking chair, but she doesn't have a ghost.' She looked at me. 'You are such a wimp, sometimes.'

'I wonder if it's the actual chair where they found the old lady?' Fern said. She held her camera up to her eye. 'Should I wait for the ghost to come back, or should I just take a picture right now?'

'Take a picture right now,' I said. I looked over my shoulder. Maybe the ghost was using the bathroom. Maybe she'd come dragging her dead old bones back here any minute now.

Arrrgh!

Cindy, pull yourself together!

Ghosts don't need to use the bathroom!

Cre-e-e-eak!

The sudden sound came from above us. We all looked up.

Creak-crik. Creak-crik. Creak-crik.

It was like someone was walking slowly across the floor in the room directly above us.

Gulp!

Well, actually, *gulp* doesn't really cover it: unless you imagine the kind of gulp that you would gulp if you were trying to swallow a basketball whole.

And then *IT* happened.

Now I know you probably think I'm kind of over-jumpy when it comes to ghosts, but Stacy isn't over-jumpy, and Pippa isn't over-jumpy, and Fern sure isn't over-jumpy.

But when *IT* happened – all four of us jumped clear of the floor and screamed at the tops of our voices.

IT?

Well, actually, *IT* was two things – two *terrible* things that happened at the same time.

A really awful groany voice came moaning from across the room. And at the same time the rocking chair began to rock. Honest to gosh! Cross my heart and hope to be buried up to my neck in a big pit and smeared with honey and left for the termites to eat! That awful old rocking chair began to rock backwards and forwards, and at exactly the same time a horrible voice began to groan and moan.

'Grahhhhh . . . gruuuurrrrhhhh . . . greeeeeeee . . . grarrrrgh!' Just like that!

Can you *imagine*?

Well, that was too much even for Fern to deal with! In fact, she almost trampled me to death as she stampeded to the front door.

All I can remember of the next few seconds was a lot of arms and legs and frightened faces and yelling and screeching and pushing and shoving to get out of there.

Somehow Fern managed to yank the front door open and we all went tumbling out into the open.

We grabbed our bikes and didn't stop pedalling until we were at least four thousand miles away from the old house.

Well – almost!

We kept right on going until we got to Maynard Park.

We bought ourselves some ice-cream at the kiosk in the park. The ice-cream helped to calm us down. When we were all completely calm, we headed back to my house. I grabbed a two-pint tub of chocolate-chip out of the freezer and we went up to my room to calm ourselves down some more.

81

'It was the wind,' Stacy said. 'I'm positive that it was just the wind.'

'Exactly,' Pippa said. 'And old houses creak all the time. It's what old houses do.'

'I'm not even sure the chair *really* moved,' Fern said. 'I think maybe it was just a trick of the light, you know?' She nodded. 'In fact, the more I think about it, the more I'm totally sure that the chair didn't move at all.' She looked around at us. 'Did any of you guys actually see the chair move?'

'I was looking up at the ceiling,' Pippa said. 'I don't exactly remember seeing the chair move.'

'I don't see how it *could* have moved,' Stacy said. 'Chairs can't move on their own. I think you're right, Fern – it was just a trick of the light. That was all it was. The wind making noises that sounded like moaning – the old house just creaking the way old houses do – and a total trick of the light which made it look like the rocking chair started rocking.' Stacy laughed – not totally convincingly, to my mind. 'It just goes to show how people's imaginations can play tricks on them, huh? What do you think, Cindy?'

'I completely agree,' I said. 'We just let our imaginations go wild. There are no ghosts!' I began to mutter to myself. 'Therearenoghosts-

therearenoghosts-therearenoghosts . . .'

'When are you going to come out of that closet?' Fern asked.

'Soon,' I said.

'There's one big bad thing about all of this,' Fern said. 'We don't have a picture of the rocking chair to show mega-mouth Sophie.'

'Why didn't you take a picture?' Pippa asked her. 'You had the camera ready and everything.'

'Uh . . . I guess it must have jammed,' Fern said. 'I tried to take a picture, but nothing happened. Drag, huh?'

'So . . .' Stacy said, '. . . if we're going to prove to Sophie that we were in the house . . . uh . . . I guess we need to go back in there . . . again . . . and take a picture.'

'Well, excuse me,' Pippa said. 'The way I recall it, the four of us agreed to go in there, right? And we *went* in there. Mission accomplished, if you ask me! It was Fern who agreed to take a picture. I don't see why the whole bunch of us should have to go all the way back over there again just because one of us didn't do what she said she was going to do.'

'I agree,' I said. 'I totally agree with Pippa. Is there any ice-cream left?'

Stacy handed me the almost-empty tub in through the closet door.

'I see,' Fern said. 'You're chickening out, is that it?'

'Not at all!' Pippa said with dignity. 'I said I'd go in the house, and I went in the house. That whole taking-a-picture business is down to you, Fern. It wasn't my idea.'

'Let's vote on whether we all go back together,' Stacy said. 'Or whether Fern goes back on her own.'

'Oh, right!' Fern said. 'That sounds totally fair and reasonable, I don't think!'

'Hands up who wants us *all* to go back,' Stacy said. I jammed my hands down on the floor of the closet, just so there was no mistaking the way I wanted to vote.

'OK,' Stacy said. 'That's one vote for us all going back. Now, hands up everyone who thinks it's Fern's fault that she didn't take the picture, and that she should go back there on her own.'

I stuck my hand out through the closet door.

'Right,' Stacy said. 'That's three votes for Fern going back on her own.'

'Big fix!' Fern grumbled.

'That's how democracy works, Fern,' Pippa said. 'One person one vote.'

There was a short silence. Then I heard Fern snort. Then I heard someone stomp off to the door.

84

'I'll see you guys later,' Fern said. '*Maybe.*'

The door slammed.

'Wow!' I thought. 'She's really going to go back there on her own. Talk about *brave!*'

Now, I know we had all been trying really hard to convince ourselves that nothing actually happened back there, but I for one was not *completely* convinced that it was all the wind and the creaky old house and tricks of the light.

And I don't care what the rest of the guys said – I saw that darned chair *move!*

Pippa's voice broke the silence after Fern had gone. 'Uh . . . guys,' she said. 'How long do you think we should leave it before we start worrying about her? Not that there's anything to worry about, of course.'

'Of course not,' Stacy said. 'But I know what you mean, Pippa. Fern might get . . . uh . . . lost . . . or something. Or . . . or she might get a flat tyre and need some help. These things happen.' She coughed. 'Now then, it took us about fifteen minutes to get over there. So, give her half an hour to get there and back. Say, five minutes to get into the house, take the snap and get out again. So, I figure we don't need to worry about her for . . . oh . . . forty minutes.'

'Not that we need to start worrying about her *after* forty minutes,' Pippa said. 'It's not like anything's going to happen to her.'

'No. Exactly,' Stacy said. 'What could happen? No way is the house haunted.'

'No way,' Pippa agreed. There was a short pause. 'So . . . we call the cops after forty minutes, right?'

'Right!'

I heard my bedroom door burst open. 'Uh . . . I've just noticed that my camera is broken,' Fern said, stomping across the floor. 'There's no point in me going all the way over there with a broken camera, is there?'

'I guess not,' Pippa said.

'Let me see it,' Stacy said. 'Maybe I could fix it for you.'

'No, that's OK,' Fern said. 'It's completely bust. It's totally beyond repair. There's no point in even looking at it.'

'What exactly isn't working?' Pippa asked.

'Exactly *nothing* is working, OK?' Fern said – sounding like she was talking between gritted teeth. 'It's *kaput*. Done for. Finished! It's as dead as a doughnut.'

'Maybe the battery is dead,' Pippa suggested.

'I'll check it out,' Fern said. 'But in the meantime, it isn't working, OK?'

'So, what do we do about Sophie now we can't take a picture of the rocking chair?' Stacy asked. 'She's really going to make a big deal out of this, you know.'

'I have a cunning and subtle plan to deal with Sophie,' Fern said. 'If she gets in our faces about not going to the haunted house, I'll threaten to rip her arms off and beat her to death with them.'

'Yes,' Pippa said. 'I can see how that might work.'

'So,' Fern said. 'What say we forget all about that dumb haunted house?'

'What haunted house is that?' Pippa said.

'Right!'

'Cindy?' Stacy said. 'Do you want to come out of the closet and join us for further discussions about our sleepover?'

I got out of the closet.

'One question, guys,' I said. 'Do we really really really want to make it a super-scary freakadelic horrorfest kind of a sleepover party after all? Only, I was just . . . uh . . . wondering whether that kind of thing isn't maybe a little . . . uh . . . childish. Know what I mean?'

'What about *Creepshow*?' Pippa said.

'Oh, yeah, we watch *Creepshow*, for sure!' I said 'But . . . maybe . . . afterwards, we could watch something a little different. Like a Disney cartoon or a comedy movie, or something like that. You know, something funny and cheerful and fun and happy and not . . . uh

. . . *scary* at all.'

'An excellently excellent idea!' Stacy said extremely quickly.

'Yup. That's gotten my vote!' Fern said.

'Mine too!' Pippa said.

'Excellent!' I said. 'So, let's pick a really nice, chirpy, cheerful, happy-go-lucky kind of a movie.'

Of course, we were all totally utterly and completely convinced that the boarded-up old house on the corner of Fairview and Halifax was not in the tiniest bit haunted. All the same, like I said to the guys, a scary sleepover party is not exactly the kind of thing that four grown-up and sophisticated young ladies like us should be getting into.

I'm telling you: scary sleepovers are definitely last year's thing!

Looking back, I guess that if I'd had half a brain, I would have suspected the next morning at breakfast that something sneaky was being hatched. Denny said something that should have rung little alarm bells – something about ghosts – but it didn't ring any little alarm bells. It's kind of annoying not even having half a brain! I'd really like to be smart. Not necessarily smart like Pippa, 'cos her kind of smart is pretty uscless on a day-to-day basis. I mean, how often do people come up to you in the street and ask if you know the capital of Ohio or the average rainfall in Venezuela? Not too often, I'll tell you – and that's the kind of useless junk Pippa's head is crammed with! The kind of smart I'd like would be the kind of smart Stacy has.

Stacy says I'm cute and she's smart, so between us we make one whole smart and cute person – which is why, according to Stacy, we should keep together for the rest of our lives.

I'll go along with that. Except for the fact that there are actually *two* of us, and if the two of us make *one* smart and cute person, we must also make one not-so-cute person who is also pretty dumb. Sad!

Anyway, I was telling you about breakfast the next morning.

The twins were fighting over who got to look for the little plastic model Splaarg in the newly opened cereal box. While Mom's back was turned, the pair of them had that box ripped wide open and they were struggling to get their arms right down inside to feel for the free Splaarg. Chocolate-coated cornflakes were flying everywhere while they did battle. It was like a regular cornflake blizzard.

'Twins!' Mom yelled. 'Cut that out!'

'It was Denny!'

'It was Bob!'

'I don't care who it was!' Mom roared. 'Quit fighting.'

'But the *Splaarg*!' Denny said.

'You guys ought to be fed in the backyard,' I said crossly, brushing chocolate-coated cornflakes off my sweater. 'In a big trough, like the pigs you both are!'

'Cindy! Don't call your brothers names!' Mom said.

'Mom!' Bob squeaked. 'You promised I

could have the next model! You *said*! Denny got the model of the Splaarg Space-bike from the last packet!'

Dad looked around the side of his newspaper. 'I guess there's no chance of you two guys *sharing*?'

Denny and Bob stared at him.

'No, I thought not,' Dad said, vanishing back behind the newspaper.

'Ha!' Denny said suddenly. 'Got it!' He whipped his arm out of the cornflakes pack, sending a great big fountain of cornflakes into the air. I could see the odd green tentacle sticking out of his fist. 'Finders keepers!'

'That does it!' Mom howled. She snatched the Splaarg out of Denny's hand and crammed it into her pocket. 'There! That's settled! I get the model!'

'Way to go, Mom,' I said, picking chocolate-coated cornflakes out of my hair.

The twins were devastated. (That's a Pippa word meaning totally upset.)

'Mo-o-o-o-om!' they hollered.

'Too late!' Mom said heartlessly. 'Splaarg is going to be heading off on an exciting mission to the office with me today. He can sit on my desk and scare people off.' She frowned at the twins. 'If you're very good, I might let you have him at the end of the week. We'll see. Now, clear that cereal up. And no throwing it all away! You're going to eat that gunk! All of it!' She wandered out of the kitchen, muttering something about idiot cereal manufacturers who put free gifts right at the bottom of the packet.

'Car in ten minutes,' Dad said, folding his newspaper and strolling out of the kitchen. Dad was on the school run that morning.

I did my best to ignore the goofs – but they turned scooping up the spilled cereal into a cornflake-throwing fight and I got hit in the eye by a bad shot.

'Will you two quit it?' I yelled.

Denny laughed. 'Or else what?'

'Or else I'll marmelise you both!'

'Ooooh, scary,' Bob giggled.

'You'd be surprised how scary I can be!' I growled, trying to look as scary as possible; which – to be honest – isn't very scary at all, unfortunately.

'What? Like, as scary as a ghost?' Denny sniggered. 'As scary as an old lady ghost in a haunted house?'

I stared at them. '*What?*' I snapped.

'Been in any good haunted houses recently?' Denny asked.

'What's it to you?' I asked.

'Nuffin',' Denny said. 'Only I thought you

and your dumb friends were talking about going to that old lady's haunted house, that's all.'

'Yeah,' I snarled. 'And you only know about that because you were listening at my door!'

'Was not!' Denny said. 'I lost a button off my shirt! I was looking for it, that was all. Anyway, you're all too scared to go look at a haunted house, if you want to know what I think.'

'Huh!' I snorted. 'Since when have you started thinking?'

'If you and your dumb friends did go to a haunted house,' Denny scoffed, 'I bet you'd all run away even if you only heard a little *mouse*!'

'Yeah,' Bob added. 'Or a tiny little fly!'

Har har har! Har-de-harr harr – *bonk*! That 'bonk' was me laughing so hard my head fell off!

'Or a wiggly worm!' Denny cackled. 'An itsy-bitsy wiggly worm!'

'A weenie termite!'

I got up and grabbed the juice carton.

They fled.

Denny's irritating face reappeared through the kitchen door. 'Or a teenie-weenie little flea!'

I threatened to throw the carton at his head, and he vanished.

I guess what really annoyed me, was that

they weren't entirely wrong. We had panicked. We had panicked big time.

'Oh, sure,' Sophie said. 'Like, I just *so* believe you guys went into the house! It just sounds so totally likely.'

'It's true!' Stacy said. 'We went right into the house, just like we said we would.'

'Yeah, yeah, yeah!'

'We *did*!' Pippa shrieked.

Sophie folded her arms and gave us the most smug, self-satisfied look I've ever seen on a person's face. 'So, where are those promised pictures, then?' she asked.

'The camera jammed,' Fern said.

'Oh, the camera jammed, did it?' Sophie said. 'Well, how *convenient*.'

'It wasn't convenient at all,' Stacy said. 'For your information, it was completely inconvenient. I really wish we had some pictures – 'cos I'd like to cram them right up your nose!'

'Well, maybe the ghost made the camera go wrong,' Sophie said. 'Maybe the ghost spooked your camera, Fern.' She looked at us from under half-lowered eyelids. 'That is, if you were ever in the house at all – which I totally doubt!'

'We were!' Pippa howled.

'Huh!'

Fern stepped forwards. 'I think I can resolve this disagreement,' she said in a cool, quiet, calm voice. 'Could I have a private word with you?' she said to Sophie. 'I do hate these silly arguments, don't you?'

'I don't see –' Sophie began.

Fern's look shut her up. We were in the hall where our lockers are kept. Fern pointed over to an empty corner.

'Would you like to step over there for a moment,' she said. 'If you're not too busy, and if you don't mind, that is?'

'Well, actually . . .'

Fern just linked her arm with Sophie's and towed her away.

Fern is amazing! Sophie is really big – she's half a head taller than Fern at least, and she's pretty beefy – but Fern just towed her across the hall like a tug leading a tanker out of dock.

Stacy and Pippa and I looked at one another. Then we looked at Fern and Sophie.

Fern was whispering into Sophie's ear. Sophie's eyes got rounder and rounder. She looked at Fern and we could see her go 'gulp!' from right across the hall.

'Is that OK, then?' Fern said. 'Do we have a deal?'

'Yes,' Sophie said.

They came back to us.

Sophie glanced at Fern. Fern smiled back at her.

'I believe you, guys,' Sophie said. 'I believe you went into the haunted house.'

'And?' Fern said.

'And I think you're all really brave,' she added. She took another look at Fern. 'I have to go to the bathroom now,' she said.

And then she skedaddled.

We looked at Fern.

'What did you *say* to her?' Pippa asked.

'Oh, nothing much,' Fern said lightly. 'I just mentioned to her that if she didn't play ball, I'd start a rumour that she was seen making out with Dennis Piblock around the back of the gym.' She grinned. 'I said I'd tell everyone that she has a total *crush* on him!'

We all shuddered. That was some threat. Dennis Piblock is the horriblest boy in the entire school. He's the absolute *pits*.

The bell went for registration. We followed Fern to Homeroom.

Boy, I'll tell you – there are times when I'm really glad Fern is on our side!

I figured that was going to be the last we'd hear of Old Miss Ugg and her haunted rocking chair.

That was what I figured.

I figured wrong!

10

Something surprising happened at breakfast the following morning.

'Do we *have* to go to Grammy's this weekend?' Denny asked.

Mom and Dad looked at him. I looked at him. Talk about unexpected!

'But you love it over at Grammy's,' Mom said.

'Well . . . yeah . . . I know . . .' Denny said.

'You get to sit up late watching TV,' Dad said. 'You get to eat as much candy and as many packs of potato chips as your stomachs can cope with. More than your stomachs can cope with, in fact. And Grammy always buys you presents. You get totally spoilt to pieces!'

Bob nodded.

'Well . . . yeah . . . I know . . .' Denny said again. 'I don't mean I don't want to go stay with Grammy at *all*. I just wish we were going next weekend instead of this weekend, that's all.' He blinked at Mom. 'Couldn't you call

Grammy and say we'd like to go over there next weekend instead?'

'Grammy won't mind,' Bob said.

Mom sat down and stared carefully at the twins. 'What's all this about?' she asked.

'Nuffin',' Denny said.

I knew! 'They want to be here on Saturday night so they can mess up my sleepover!' I said. 'Mom! Don't let 'em.'

'Well?' Mom asked them.

'Why would we want to mess up Cindy's dumb sleepover?' Bob said.

'I'd forgotten all about Cindy's dumb sleep-over,' Denny added.

'Is Cindy having a *sleepover*?' Bob said. (That's what is known as laying it on with a trowel!)

'Give me one good reason why you shouldn't go to Grammy's on Saturday,' Mom said.

Denny looked at her. 'I don't think I'm going to feel very well,' he said. 'It would be awful for Grammy if I went over there and I wasn't very well and she had to look after me and I couldn't even get out of bed, 'cos I felt so sick.'

'What kind of not very well are you planning on feeling?' Dad asked.

Denny frowned thoughtfully. 'I think I've

caught a cold. Ricky Norman sits right behind me and he's been sneezing over me all week.'

Mom 'tut-tutted' and shook her head. 'Well, I'm shocked that Ricky Norman's mom could be so irresponsible as to let him attend school with a bad cold. In fact, I'm going to call her right this minute and give her a piece of my mind. I have her number somewhere from the PTA committee.'

'Wait!' Denny squeaked. 'It wasn't Ricky Norman, now I come to think about it. It wasn't Ricky Norman who was doing all the sneezing.'

'No?' Mom said. 'Then who was it?'

'I forget,' Denny said. 'I mean, I never saw who it was. They were sitting behind me.' He spread his hands out. 'It could have been any-one.'

'Bob?' Mom asked. 'Do you know who this phantom cold-germ spreader is?'

'I just heard sneezing,' he said. 'I didn't see who sneezed.'

Dad was gazing at them. 'Someone in your class has been sitting behind you and sneezing all week, and you don't know who it is?' he said.

Denny nodded and Bob shook his head. They looked at each other. Denny shook his head and Bob nodded. They looked at each other again. They both nodded.

'Then I'd better call the school and find out,' Mom said.

'No!' Denny squeaked. 'It wasn't in school. I remember now! It was somewhere else, wasn't it, Bob?'

'Yeah. It was at Leo's house.'

'No! It wasn't,' Denny said. 'It was . . . out in the street . . . somewhere. Yeah, that's where it was.'

Dad looked at Mom. 'This sounds serious,' he said. 'If there's someone following the twins around and sneezing over them, I think the police should be informed.'

'Nooooo!' Denny wailed.

Mom gave them her special look. (I've mentioned Mom's special look before, I think.) 'What's all this about?' she said. 'And give me a break with the sneezing, please! Why don't you want to go to Grammy's this weekend?'

'Dunno,' Denny muttered.

'Right! Then you're going!' Mom said. 'End of discussion!'

A few minutes later I got the twins to myself for a few moments. 'I know why you don't want to go over to Grammy's Saturday night!' I said. 'You want to stay here so you can ruin my party! Well, tough luck, guys, 'cos it's not going to happen! You're totally *going* to

Grammy's, and that's the end of it! So, *nyahhh*!'

Except that it wasn't.

Do you remember a few days ago that my Dad was grumbling and complaining that he never wins any of the competitions he sends away for? (It was the same day he retrieved his lucky hat from the compost – and we all know how it got there, don't we, Mom?)

Remember that this latest competition of his was to win a weekend break for two in a swanky hotel on the shores of Lake Michigan? And remember how Mom said: 'You haven't won. Not in a million years have you won. You never win *anything*, Frank'? Remember all that?

Well, hold on to your hair-grips, folks, because a miracle was about to happen in the Spiegel household. It happened early Thursday evening.

It began normally enough.

Brring. Brring. Brring.

'Get the phone, someone,' Mom called.

I went and picked it up. 'Hello?'

'Could I speak to Frank Spiegel, please?' said a young woman from the other end.

'Just a second,' I said. Then I remembered what my mom had always told me about phone messages. 'Who can I say is calling, please?'

'My name is Laura McNaughty, from Zee-Zee Tip-Top Cereals. It's in connection with Mr Spiegel's competition entry.'

'Oh. Right.' I was kind of stunned. I didn't know Laura McNaughty from a hole in the ground – but Zee-Zee Tip-Top Cereals were the people who made the breakfast cereal with the Lake Michigan competition on the back of the packet. What did they want with my dad? Was Laura McNaughty the person who called people to tell them they hadn't won?

I went and fetched Dad from in front of a baseball game on TV.

'It's someone from the cereal company,' I told him.

I hung around while he took the call. At first he just looked kind of blank. Then a big beaming smile stretched right across his face and he yelled: 'You're kidding?' He stared at the phone. He stared at me. He did a little dance on the carpet and waved the phone in the air. 'Can I make it? Of course I can make it! I've never won anything in my entire life before! Celia! *Celia!*' He must have just about deafened the poor woman down the other end of the phone as he bellowed for Mom.

'*Frank?* What on earth –' Mom came into the hall.

'Pack your bags!' Dad yelled, dancing

around and waving the phone in the air. 'We're going to the Hotel Majestic on the shores of Lake Michigan! I won the competition! I *won*!'

Well, to cut a long story short, here's what had happened. Apparently Dad had been a runner-up in the competition – they were planning on sending him a Wild Birds of North America calendar as his prize, but at the last moment the two people who had actually won the Weekend Break had been forced to pull out.

'The guy broke his leg falling off a ladder!' Dad shrieked with laughter as he told us the full story a few minutes later. 'He was climbing up into the attic to get their suitcases, and he fell off the ladder!'

'Frank, that's not funny,' Mom said. 'That's not funny at all!'

'No,' Dad howled, rocking to and fro and slapping his knees. 'No, you're completely right. It's not funny at all.' And then he collapsed into laughter again.

'They're express-mailing the tickets to us straight away,' Dad said when he'd recovered. 'They should be here in the morning. Oh, wait until I tell the guys! I finally won something!'

'Yes, well, that's all very exciting and everything,' Mom said. 'But what exactly do you plan we do with the children while the two of us are up enjoying ourselves in the Hotel Majestic?'

Dad blinked at her. 'Grammy can come and look after them,' he said. He looked at me. 'That will be OK, won't it, honey?' Dad was so pleased and excited and overjoyed that he'd finally won something – even if it was only because some poor chump had fallen off a ladder.

'Of course it will,' I said. 'Which weekend is it for?'

'*This* one!' he yelled. 'The reservation is for *this* weekend. That's why they had to call me to check we were free.'

'Uh . . . *this* weekend?' I said. 'As in, this Saturday?'

'Yes!' he grinned at Mom. 'Isn't this just the most amazing thing that has ever happened to anyone in the entire history of the Universe?'

Mom laughed. 'Yes, Frank, I guess it is.'

'Excuse me,' I said. 'I think we already have plans for this weekend. Like, my *sleepover* for instance? And I think we'd decided that the twins would be staying over at Grammy's on Saturday night.' I looked at Dad. 'I think we decided that, didn't we?'

His face fell. 'Oh, Cindy! I forgot! I completely forgot!'

I looked at him. Mom looked at me. Dad

looked at Mom. Mom looked at him. One of Mom's eyebrows went up.

'You promised,' I said in a small voice.

Dad sucked in a great big breath, like you do just before you take a look at the result of a test you already know you've bombed in. 'I'll call them back,' he said. 'I'll tell them we can't make it after all.' He smiled weakly and patted my hair. 'You'll have your sleepover, honey, don't you worry.' On the way to the hall, he turned and tried another smile. 'Someone is in for a nice surprise!'

I looked at Mom. She was gazing at me.

'What?' I said.

'Nothing, Cindy,' she said. 'Nothing at all.'

'You promised I could have a sleepover if we all helped out with the sale,' I said quietly.

'Yes, we did,' Mom said.

'And you agreed that the twins should go over to Grammy's,' I said.

Mom nodded.

I blinked at her. 'Dad will win something else, I bet,' I said.

'I'm sure he will, honey,' Mom said.

I gulped. 'If Grammy comes over here, the twins will completely ruin my sleepover party,' I said.

'Couldn't you put it off until next weekend?' Mom asked.

'Nope,' I said. 'Next weekend Pippa is going away with her mom. And the weekend after that, Stacy won't be around. And the weekend after that, Fern has to do something. That's why we chose this weekend. Otherwise we can't have a sleepover with all of us for a *month*. For at *least* a month!' I looked at her. A little voice in the back of my head was telling me I was being totally selfish.

'Do you want me to tell Dad it's OK for you to go away?' I asked.

Mom shook her head. 'No, honey,' she said. 'I don't want you to do that at all. We promised you a sleepover party with your friends, and that the twins would be out of the way at Grammy's house. There's no reason why you should have all your plans ruined at the last minute.'

'Yes, but . . .' I sighed. 'Dad has never won anything before.'

'True,' Mom said.

'He may never win anything again for the rest of his life,' I said.

'That's a distinct possibility,' Mom said.

'Oh, heck!' I whispered.

I walked out into the hall to tell Dad not to call Laura McNaughty back. I couldn't be so selfish as to ask him to turn down the only first prize he had ever won in his whole life.

And after all, Stacy and Fern and Pippa and I would be more than a match for the twins if they started to make pests of themselves.

I mean, it's not like the house would be turned into a total battlefield on Saturday night.

11

'You do realise that the whole house will be turned into a total battlefield all night?' Stacy pointed out, really helpfully, when I told everyone the news the next morning at school.

'Cindy, what were you *thinking*?' Fern asked.

'You guys would have done exactly the same thing if you had seen the look on my dad's face,' I said. 'I *couldn't* ruin it all for him. I just couldn't.'

Fern muttered something about me being too soft for my own good.

'Guys?' I said. 'I'm really sorry. Maybe we could have the sleepover somewhere else?'

'Not at my house,' Stacy said. 'Amanda has invited the Bimbos over.'

We all shuddered. Four Bimbos were even worse than the terrible twins.

'My folks are going away overnight,' Fern said.

'My mom is planning on watching a four-and-a-half-hour opera on TV on Saturday night,' Pippa said. 'She's been looking forward to it for weeks.'

'Then I guess it's my house or we cancel,' I said.

'Look, guys,' Fern said. 'I think we're in danger of kind of over-reacting to the situation here. Denny and Bob might be the most horrible kids in the world –'

'They're not quite that bad,' I murmured. I felt like I ought to defend them just a *little*. After all, they are my brothers.

Fern ignored me. 'But the bottom line is that there are four of us and there are only two of them. And we're bigger than them. If the worst comes to the worst, we could sit on their heads till they cry Uncle.'

'Fern's right,' Stacy said. 'Let's just have a good time, right? And if the twins are pests, we'll deal with it.'

Fern thumped her fist into her hand. 'We'll mash 'em to a pulp. Two pulps.'

'Is your Grammy good at controlling them?' Pippa asked. 'I mean, she doesn't let them run totally wild, does she?'

'Uh . . . not *totally*,' I said.

'It'll be fine,' Stacy said. 'The reason they could be such a pain last time was because we were all sleeping down in the living room. This time we'll be sleeping in Cindy's room. We can lock the door. They won't be able to do a thing.'

'You're right,' I said, brightening a little. 'After all, once the door is locked, what can they do?'

Yeah – what could they do?

I decided the twins could use a little pre-sleep-over party pep-talk. I hunted them down in their room that day after school.

They were huddled up together in a corner with one of their Splaarg comics, scribbling stuff down on a note pad and giggling like a couple of stupid chimps.

They were so busy with whatever they were doing, that they didn't even notice me standing in the doorway.

I banged on the door.

'Hi, little brothers,' I said cheerfully. 'How's tricks?' I figured it was best not to come the heavy older sister with them – after all I did need them to agree a truce on Saturday night, so I didn't want to put their backs up by threatening them or being angry or anything like that. Stacy says this is called *diplomacy*.

I was amazed by the effect on the twins. They nearly shot straight through the ceiling when I spoke. Denny grabbed the comic and crammed it down behind them.

'We're not doing anything!' Bob shrieked.

'What do you want?' Denny shouted. 'What are you doing in our room? This is *our* room!'

'You can't come in,' Bob said. 'Go away!'

'All right, all right,' I said. 'Don't get your underwear in an uproar.' I grinned at them. 'What's with the comic?'

'What comic?' Denny said.

'The one you just hid,' I said.

'It's nuffin',' Denny said. 'What's it to you?'

'Nothing at all,' I said. 'I don't care what silly games you're up to.' I frowned. 'Unless you're intending to ruin my sleepover, that is.' I took a step into the room. ''Cos I think I should warn you guys, I won't like it if you try to ruin my sleepover. Get the message?'

'We're not frightened of you,' Denny said.

'Maybe not,' I said, smiling again. 'But Fern is coming over, don't forget. And I'm sure you remember what Fern did to you last time when you were being total pests.'

'Mom made her clear it all up,' Denny said. 'And she had to take our T-shirts away to have them washed.'

'True,' I agreed. 'But that won't stop her from doing something similar all over again if you make her angry.' I shook my head. 'You really don't want to get Fern mad, guys. You won't like Fern if she gets mad.'

'We're not scared of Fern,' Bob muttered, not terribly convincingly. I guess he still had a vivid memory of having a squeezy bottle of mayonnaise squirted down the back of his T-shirt. I mean, it's not the kind of experience you easily forget – especially not when it comes complete with Fern sitting right on top of you and squishing you into the carpet like a bug.

I spread my hands out. 'Here's the deal, guys: if you leave us alone on Saturday night, we'll leave you alone. How does that sound? Can we work together on this, huh? Can we act like sensible grown-up people?'

Denny and Bob looked at me.

'Is it a deal?' I asked.

'Sure,' Denny said.

'Great!' I turned to leave them to their dumb little conspiracy with their dumb little magazine.

'Hey, Cindy. Ever heard of a *poltergoose*?' Denny asked.

I turned back. 'Excuse me?'

'A *poltergoose*,' Denny said. 'It's a kind of ghost.'

'No,' I said. 'I've never heard of a poltergoose.'

Denny and Bob grinned like a pair of hungry crocs.

I put my hands on my hips. 'What?' I said.

'What's so funny all of a sudden?'

'Oh, nuffin',' Denny said. 'I just thought you might like to know what a *poltergoose* is – just in case you meet one.'

'And why exactly should I meet a *poltergoose*?' I said.

'Well, if a person has been in a haunted house,' Denny said. 'And if a person has disturbed a *ghost*, then I think it would be really useful for a person to know that ghosts *follow* people.'

I stared at him.

'What do you mean: ghosts follow people?' I asked.

Denny nodded, still grinning. 'Didn't you know?' he said. 'I thought everyone knew that. Ghosts don't like it when people go into their houses. It makes them mad. And when ghosts get mad, they follow people back to their own homes and they start behaving really badly. Really scarily.'

'They throw stuff and make horrible noises and move furniture around,' Bob said. 'You'd be frightened out of your life!'

'And angry ghosts who do stuff like that are called *poltergooses*,' Denny added. 'I thought maybe you'd want to know.'

'Why should I want to know that?' I asked, totally calmly.

Denny's grin widened. 'I thought maybe you and your dopey friends went into the haunted house,' he said.

My eyes narrowed. 'Have you been listening at my door again?' I snarled.

Denny put on his most innocent face. 'Me?' he said. 'Excuse me, but I don't listen at people's doors. Maybe you're thinking of someone else. Maybe you're thinking of one of your friends. They're the kind of people who listen at doors, if you ask me.'

'No, they're not!' I glared at him. 'And for your information,' I lied, 'we never went in the haunted house at all, so thanks for telling me about *poltergooses* and all that other junk, but I don't see what it has to do with me at all.'

Denny shrugged. 'Well, if you didn't go into the haunted house, then I guess you don't have anything to worry about,' he said. '*Poltergooses* only haunt people who have been in haunted houses.'

'Oh, shut up about *poltergooses*!' I yelled. I slammed the door on them and stomped off to my room.

Poltergooses! I mean – *please*!

What kid of a scaredy-cat idiot did my dumb twin brothers think I was? Did they really think they would be able to freak me out by making up silly stories about ghosts who follow people back to their own houses and start flinging the furniture about and groaning and grisly ghostly stuff like that?

Huh! As *if*!

'Oh, hi, Mrs Allen, could I speak to Stacy please?' I said down the phone. 'Thanks.'

I've never heard of ghosts who follow people home. Ghosts have to stay in their own houses – that's what ghosts do. They stay at home: in haunted houses. They don't *follow* people.

'Hi?'

'Oh, hi, Stacy. It's me. Now I know there are no such things as ghosts, but if there *were* such things as ghosts, do you think it would be possible for ghosts to get so mad at people who went into their haunted houses that they'd follow those people home afterwards and, kind of *haunt* them in their own houses?'

'Cindy, calm down – you sound like a total wreck. What are you talking about?'

'Have you ever heard of *poltergooses*?' I asked.

'*Poltergooses*?' Stacy said. 'Did you say *poltergooses*?'

'Uh-huh,' I said. 'I know for a fact that there's no such thing at all, but I just wondered if you'd ever heard of them.'

'I think you mean *poltergeists*,' Stacy said. 'Not poltergooses! *Poltergeists*.'

'What are *poltergeists*?' I said.

'Haven't you ever seen the movie?' Stacy asked. 'Poltergeists are ghosts who throw stuff around and move furniture and wreck stuff in people's houses.'

'Arrrrgh!' I said, completely calmly. That was exactly what Denny had told me *poltergooses* do!

12

'Poltergeists are an extremely interesting phenomenon,' Pippa said. 'For instance, did you know that they only usually appear when there's a kid in the house? A kid in their early teens.' She looked around at us. 'Kids around our age, in fact,' she said. 'Isn't that interesting?'

I sat at the table in the school cafeteria, my spoon hanging in my limp hand, caramel fudge yoghurt dripping back into the carton, my eyes popping and my mouth hanging open.

Stacy shook her head and rolled her eyes.

Fern looked at me and chuckled. 'Someone's freaking out,' she said.

'Listen, Cindy,' Stacy said. 'Your brothers were trying to scare you, is all. I don't believe that ghosts follow people around. It's not the kind of thing that ghosts do.'

'I'm not scared,' I said.

'Good,' Stacy said. 'I'm glad to hear it.' She looked at Fern. 'Have you picked a movie for us to watch on Saturday night?'

Fern pulled out a slip of paper. 'I've been through my folks' stocks, and I've whittled it down to a final four choices.' She consulted the paper. 'First off the blocks is *Saturday Night Of The Living Dead Zombies*. Second on the list is *The Grisly Ghostly Sleepover Slaughter*. Three is *My Sister Was Murdered By Spooks*. Four is –'

'Fern!' Stacy interrupted. 'Quit that! Tell us the real titles.'

But Fern was too busy pointing at me and laughing.

'I don't find that especially funny,' I said. 'You're a sick person, Fern. Sick, sick, sick!'

'Now, then, kids,' Mom said on Friday night. 'I want to have a quick word with you about how things are going to be while your dad and I are away.'

She had sat the three of us down on the couch in the living room. She was standing in front of us with her arms folded and with a stern look on her face.

'Boys? You will not interfere with your sister or her friends in any way whatsoever. You will keep completely out of their way and you will not lay traps for them or annoy them in any manner whatsoever. Is that clear?'

'Yes, Mom,' they chorused.

Good for you, Mom! You tell 'em!

I stuck my tongue out at them.

'Cindy!'

I snapped my head around. Mom was frowning at me. 'Cindy, you will not antagonise your brothers. And that includes poking your tongue out at them and calling them names.'

'Yes, but –'

'You're ten years old, Cindy,' Mom said. 'Act like it, please. I'm trusting you all to be on your very best behaviour with Grammy. I've given her strict instructions to report back to me if there's any nonsense from any of you.' She leaned closer. 'And Grammy will have our phone number at the hotel, so that if the three of you don't behave *impeccably* your dad and I will be forced to check out of our luxury hotel – and come back here to deal with you in person.' Her eyes glowed dangerously. 'Do I make myself crystal clear?'

'I'll say!' I nodded.

'We weren't planning on doing stuff to annoy Cindy anyway,' Bob said. 'It never crossed our minds.'

'Yeah!' Denny added. 'And if she's been telling stories, they're not true at all!' He glared at me. 'That was just an ordinary Splaarg comic we were looking at.'

I blinked at them.

Mom stared at them.

They gazed innocently back at Mom.

'I don't have the least idea what you're talking about,' Mom said. She wagged a finger at all of us. 'Just remember what I've told you. Any nonsense and you'll think the sky has fallen on you, got me?'

And that was the end of our little pep-talk from Mom.

I couldn't help wondering what Denny had meant about that comic. I figured he was talking about the one they'd hidden when I went into their room.

Was there something special about the comic? Something, for instance, that a big sister ought to know about?

Just to be on the safe side, I snuck into their room later that night while they were having their baths. I went right through their heap of comics, but I couldn't find anything much in there – not unless you're really into Splaarg the Space Mutant, of course.

Still – it was strange: why would Denny make such a point of telling Mom that it was just an *ordinary* comic, unless actually it *wasn't* an ordinary comic?

Oh, well – I had better things to think about. Grammy would be coming over early in the morning, and first thing on the agenda, once we'd shipped Mom and Dad off to the Hotel Majestic, was a trip to the supermarket in the mall to buy provisions for our sleepover.

Grammy lives all on her own with two fat cats and seventeen birds in a big house on the other side of town. Grandpa doesn't live with her any more, but they're still really good friends. Grandpa lives in a log cabin in a place called Saskatchewan. That's up in Canada, in case you didn't know. Grammy says that Grandpa always had a 'yearning for the snowy wastes of the north'. When they were younger, Grammy used to go up to Canada with him for vacations, and they used to climb mountains together and canoe down rivers and do stunning stuff like that. But Grammy says that as she got older she didn't feel quite so much like climbing mountains and whitewater rafting any more, so she'd send Grandpa off to Saskatchewan on his own while she stayed home, all cosy and warm with her two big tortoiseshell cats and her seventeen cockatiels. And one time, Grandpa didn't come back after the vacation was over.

They call each other almost every day and they write long letters to one another, and Grammy says they're still totally in love – but in an *unusual* kind of a way. They see each other on special family occasions, and Grandpa comes down to Four Corners once or twice a year for vacations. Weird, huh? But Mom says they're both happy, and that's all that matters. And I guess that's true.

Grammy arrived early on Saturday morning in her old pick-up. Every time Mom claps eyes on that car she rolls her eyes and shakes her head. She thinks Grammy should buy a new one. Grammy says cars are like slippers: where's the sense in changing cars just when your old car starts to fit snugly?

The boys were all over Grammy the moment she stepped out of the car. They knew she'd have presents for them. Grammy reminds me of an early pioneer: she doesn't dye or style her hair – she just ties it back and lets it hang down. And she doesn't wear snazzy modern clothes either. She marches about in big floral print dresses and a denim jacket that's falling all to pieces.

Fern says my grammy is the oldest hippy in town.

Grammy had baked a whole batch of cakes and cookies and brownies for us. And she had brought over some of her special home-made jam and bottled fruit and a big two-gallon jug of home-made lemonade.

It took a long time to ferry all the stuff into the kitchen.

Then Mom started reminding Grammy where everything was, until Grammy picked up Mom's overnight bag and more or less pushed her out of the house.

'Go!' she said. 'Enjoy yourselves! We'll do just fine.'

Dad brought the car out of the garage and Mom got in, still calling out last-minute instructions. We stood in the doorway, hugging Grammy and waving as Mom and Dad drove off.

We helped Grammy settle in. The twins fought to take her bag up to the spare bedroom. I told her all my plans for the sleepover while we were in the kitchen, transferring all Grammy's goodies into the cupboards. Of course, we had to try one or two things as we went along.

In the end the four of us had the most amazing late breakfast, and by the time it came to washing the dishes we could hardly move because of how much we'd eaten.

I love Grammy to pieces!

Saturday: The Plan.

After lunch, the twins went over to their pal Leo's house for the rest of the day. I thought it was a big shame that they couldn't stay there overnight, but there was a major problem with that: they had stayed overnight at Leo's house two weeks ago and his mom still hadn't recovered from the experience.

Grammy and I drove over to the supermarket. Mom had left Grammy enough money to pay for everything. The guys and I had spent a lot of time on the food and drink list – I mean, we didn't want to all settle down in front of the TV that night only to have someone suddenly say: 'Where's the toffee-coated popcorn?' 'Oh, no! We forgot the toffee-coated popcorn.' You know the kind of thing that can happen if you don't plan things properly.

The only thing wrong was that Mom had insisted on checking our list over, and she'd crossed out about a third of the stuff we'd written down. Moms, huh?

Later in the afternoon, when Grammy and I had gotten back from the supermarket, Stacy and Fern and Pippa arrived.

'How come you brought your camera?' I asked Fern when she came marching in through the front door with her overnight bag across her shoulder. She had the camera swinging around her neck on its strap. 'I thought you said it was broken?'

'It got better,' Fern said. 'I thought it would

124

be real neat to take some pictures of our sleep-over.'

'Yes, that's a great idea,' I said. 'But what do you mean: it got better? Who fixed it for you?'

'No one,' Fern said. 'It just got . . . better.' She shrugged. 'Amazing, huh?'

'Hmm!' Do you know, if I wasn't totally convinced that Fern is completely fearless and brave, I'd be really suspicious that her camera had never been bust at all, but that she just pretended it had been bust in order to get out of going back to the haunted house.

Rats – and I was trying really hard not to think about the haunted house!

Fern had also brought over a small selection of happy and cheerful videos for us to watch after *Creepshow*.

The problem was that the guys weren't all that interested in helping me to decide which happy and cheerful videos we were going to watch later. All they wanted to talk about was *Creepshow*.

While we were getting everything ready for the show, Fern and Stacy talked through all the trailer-snippets we'd seen in the past few weeks, trying to guess which would be the opening episode.

'It'll be the one with the swamp monster

living in the sewers under the town,' Fern said.

'No, it'll be the one with the vampire librarian,' Pippa said.

'No way,' Stacy said. 'It'll be the one with the haunted mad killer cat – I betcha!'

We moved the couch closer to the TV, and Pippa closed the curtains, even though it wasn't really dark yet. She said it would help with the ambience.

'With the *ambulance*?' Fern said. 'What ambulance?'

'Not ambulance! *Ambience*!' Pippa repeated. 'It means *atmosphere*.'

'So why didn't you say so?' Fern asked.

Pippa just sighed and shook her head.

We put snacks onto dishes and plates and spread them all around the couch so they'd be within easy reach. (This was so we didn't have to go searching for something to eat right in the middle of the show.)

Grammy heated up pizza slices and Stacy made sure the TV reception was totally perfect.

'It's a little fuzzy,' Pippa said, regarding the screen with a critical eye. 'Hand me the remote, Stacy. I'll fix it.'

'Don't you dare!' I screeched. 'Don't let her *near* it, Stacy!'

That was the last thing we needed: Pippa the Jinx trying to improve the picture. That was a certain sure way of missing the show.

There were only a few minutes to go before the show started. We gathered in the living room.

Stacy insisted that we turn the lights down low. Fern suggested we watch the programme by candlelight, but Grammy couldn't find any candles. (Phew!) We had all our snacks and drinks to hand, and the four of us crammed together on the couch. Grammy sat in the armchair.

I felt something moving on my shoulder. It crept stealthily towards my neck. I shrieked. Fern burst out laughing. It was her hand! I pointed out that if she did that again, I'd be forced to kill her completely dead.

Creepshow started.

It began with the screen going black. Then there was a blood-curdling scream and the camera seemed to be flying through the air while ghosts and goblins and witches and boggarts swarmed about. The scene changed to a big old house and we zoomed in through an upstairs window into this big dark old cobwebby attic. The show's host, a pale, blackhaired witchy kind of a woman called *Walpurgia* sat in an old rocking chair, stroking a black cat with one long, skinny hand with long, curved green fingernails.

'Welcome back, dear viewers,' she whispered in a creepy voice. 'Welcome back to the weird world of the Unknown.' The camera zoomed in on her big black eyes. 'Have you ever wondered what it would be like if you incurred the deep and abiding wrath of a ghost? Have you ever considered the consequences of making a ghost angry?' Her head shook slowly. 'Follow me, dear viewers, and let me tell you the tale of Kelsey Mottwangler. The tale of a man who went alone to a haunted house and who took away from that house a great deal more than he had bargained for.' There was a ghastly shriek of laughter. 'I have called this charming little fable: "The Ghoul That Came To Stay".'

13

I guess you want to know what happened on *Creepshow*. Well, it all started with this guy called Kelsey Mottwangler walking into a real estate office, looking to buy a house. The guy in the office said there was a property available right away at a very reasonable price. But then the guy told Kelsey Mottwangler that there were rumours that the house was haunted – which was why it was for sale so cheap.

Well, Kelsey Mottwangler said he didn't believe in ghosts (he obviously didn't know he was in *Creepshow*!). He took the key from the guy and arranged to go view the house.

Well, just after Kelsey went into the haunted house and saw the ghost at the top of the stairs, I kind of *hid* behind the couch. Not that covering my eyes and hiding did me much good, 'cos Fern and the rest kept yelling out what was happening.

'Cindy! Cindy!' Fern yelled. 'You don't

know what you're missing! The ghost has followed the guy home and he doesn't know it.'

Rrring.

'That was his front doorbell, Cindy,' Pippa called back to me. There was a shriek from everyone. 'Monsters!' Pippa yelled. 'Cindy! Look! He opened the door and there are *monsters* on his doorstep! EE-owowowowow-yik!'

The poor guy's entire house turned against him. The stair carpet came loose and tripped him down the stairs. A window whacked down on his head. Knives and forks and other kitchen stuff came alive and went whizzing past his ears as he ran for cover.

I could hear all the screaming and whizzing and slicing and thudding noises even though I had my ears covered. And Stacy was nice enough to lean over the back of the couch and yank my hands away from my ears to tell me how the guy's toothpaste turned into a poisonous snake just as he squirted it onto his brush.

After spending the entire day fighting off evil ghost-things and homicidal cutlery, the poor guy staggered up to bed.

'I bet something really grisly happens to him in bed,' Fern said with relish.

I listened to screaming and howling and horrible squishing, squooging noises.

'Ew! The bedcovers are squeezing the life

out of him!' Stacy yelled.

'Told you so!' Fern crowed. 'That guy is dead meat, I'm telling you.'

'He'll get out of it somehow,' Pippa said.

A split second later there was a fearful choking, gurgling noise and then a really awful silence.

'What happened?' I called.

'He didn't get out of it,' Stacy said. 'He's totally dead.'

'There's blood everywhere, Cindy,' Fern said. 'You'd love it!'

And that was the end of Kelsey Mottwangler. But it wasn't the end of the story, 'cos what happened next was that the scene changed to a young woman in that same real estate office, looking for a house. And the guy in the office said, 'We have this property, going for a very reasonable price . . .' And the guy said, 'I have to be honest with you, there are stories that the place is haunted.'

The woman just laughed and said she didn't believe in ghosts. She took the key and said she'd go visit the house. Which is *exactly* what Kelsey Mottwangler had said, so, although the programme ended just as she was opening the front door of the house, there were no prizes for guessing what happened to *her* next!

'Well!' Grammy declared. 'Wasn't that fun?'

The closing credits of *Creepshow* faded away with a final blood-curdling, goose-fleshing, hair-raising, toe-curling, nose-tweaking, heart-stopping, breath-taking knee-wobbling, stomach-churning *SCREEEEEECH!*

'Coo-oo-ool,' Fern breathed.

'Excellently excellent!' Stacy murmured.

'Wow,' Pippa said.

'I think we could all use a good fortifying snack after all that excitement,' Grammy said. 'What do you girls say?'

'More pizza?' Fern suggested.

'Leave it to me,' Grammy said. She got up and went off to the kitchen.

Stacy turned around on the couch and leaned over the back.

'How's it going, Cindy?' she asked, peering down at me.

'Fine,' I said.

'You can come out now,' Pippa said. 'It's over.'

I stood up and came around to the front of the couch. I sat down. 'Uh . . . what movie are we going to watch now?' I asked.

Fern dumped a bunch of videos in my lap. They all looked really fluffy and cheerful and unthreatening. 'This one!' I said. '*Summer Fun For The Terronvale Twins*. I haven't seen that one for ages.'

We started to watch the movie. The Terronvale Twins were at Summer Camp. The sky was blue and everyone was happy. Ahhh!

'Which part of *Creepshow* did you think was the scariest?' Stacy asked.

'The scene where the guy's toothbrush turned into a snake and got a hold of his tongue and ripped it out by the roots,' Fern said, gurgling with laughter. 'Definitely.'

'I thought the scene where the bedcovers came alive and strangled him was pretty neat,' Pippa said.

'And what about when he was sitting there watching TV and the doorbell rang,' Stacy said. 'And when he opened the door there were those horrible, hideous, disgusting *things* on the doorstep. Brrr!'

'Guys,' I said. 'Can we discuss this later, please? I'm trying to follow the movie.'

'Yeah,' Fern said. 'Let's wait until we're all up in bed in the dark.'

'No!' I squeaked. 'I meant *later* than that.'

'How much later?' Stacy asked.

'Maybe we could have a reunion when we're, uh, forty years old?' I suggested.

'Cindy, don't take this the wrong way,' Fern said. 'But you are the scarediest scaredy-cat in the world. It was just a TV programme! What do you think's going to happen? Do you think the front doorbell's gonna ring, huh? Huh? And do you think there'll be two horrible hideous disgusting monsters out there when you go answer the door?'

'No,' I said. 'Of course not.'

'Exactly!' Fern said. 'Of course not!'

Ri-i-i-i-i-ing!

'Arrrgh!'

'Will someone get the door, please?' Grammy called from the kitchen. 'That'll be Denny and Bob.'

Fern laughed. 'Well, I guess I was wrong! There *are* two monsters out there!'

Stacy let the twins in. Leo's dad had dropped them off. It was really past their bedtime, but Grammy put some extra pizza slices in the oven for them and told them they could stay up and watch TV if they wanted to.

They took one look at *Summer Fun For The Terronvale Twins* and both went 'Yuuuurkkkk! No way!'

'It's that or nothing,' I told them. 'Anyway, you should be in bed at this time of night.'

Grammy came in with a couple of plates loaded with pizza slices.

'Can we eat up in our room?' asked Denny.

'I don't see why not,' Grammy said.

The twins aren't usually allowed to eat up in

134

their room because of sticky messes on the carpet and in their beds and because of the way plates and knives and forks and cups seem to vanish for ever up there. But I didn't mention this to Grammy, because I figured that it would be a whole lot better for us if the twins were safely shut away upstairs and out of our hair.

'Can we play on the computer for a while?' Bob asked.

'For a little while,' Grammy said. 'Not too loud, though, boys.'

'Oh, no,' Denny said. 'We won't make a single sound. Promise.'

They both grabbed at pizza slices and zipped upstairs.

The four of us looked at one another. Maybe the twins weren't going to be a pain after all. Maybe we were going to be able to have our sleepover without any running battles up and down the house. Maybe wonders will never cease!

Well, to cut a long story short, we watched the movie with Grammy, and by the end of the movie, we were feeling a little peckish again – like you do when you know you're going to be up chatting with your pals most of the night. So we fetched ourselves a whole heap of food from the kitchen and watched another movie. It was called *A Pony For July*. You should watch it if you get the chance, it was really exciting and sad and thrilling and funny, and it had a great ending where everything came right for the heroine and her beloved pony in the last couple of minutes.

Grammy started yawning two-thirds of the way through the movie, and by the end she was dozing in her chair.

'I'm for the wooden hill to Bedfordshire!' Grammy said as the credits rolled over a long-shot of Donna Bradshaw riding her pony Trixie over the fields of her New England farm.

We decided we may as well go up, too.

I was still kind of puzzled by the fact that we hadn't heard a single sound from the twins. Not even the usual *Zrrp-zrrp-bukka-bukka-kapow!* racket that you get when they play their Splaarg games on the computer. They were being as quiet as mice up there.

In fact, as Stacy put it, they were being 'as quiet as mice who are wearing felt slippers and who have taken a vow of silence and have bad laryngitis, and who have been tied into their beds with sacks over their heads packed with cotton wool.'

'I call that kind of suspicious,' Fern said while the two of us were in the bathroom cleaning our teeth. 'What are they up to, that's what I'd like to know?'

'What do you mean?' I said.

'Well, my mom always says that when I'm *too* quiet – when I'm not making a *sound* – that's when she knows I'm up to something sneaky.' Fern nodded, foaming at the mouth with toothpaste. 'And she's usually totally correct.'

Maybe Fern was right. I decided to check it out. I crept along to the twins' room and listened at the door.

There wasn't a sound. There wasn't a peep out of them.

I quietly opened the door. The room was in darkness.

Amazing! They had put themselves to bed without having to be told twenty million times.

Mind you, I wasn't so gullible as to think they hadn't laid some traps for us. My room would need to be carefully examined.

We took up heaps of emergency rations for the night. I have a double-size bed, so there was room in there for Stacy and me. Pippa and Fern had a mattress made up on the floor.

We checked the beds and the surrounding areas really thoroughly for booby-traps. There didn't seem to be any.

'Curiouser and curiouser,' Pippa said.

'Perhaps they aren't going to bother messing with us, after all?'

'I'll lock the door, all the same,' I said.

I turned the key. 'There! Now they can't make any sneak attacks on us in the middle of the night.'

We got into our PJs and clambered into bed. The only light was from my bedside lamp.

'Fern, quit it!' Pippa said.

'It wasn't me,' Fern giggled. 'It was a great huge leggy spider.'

'Fine!' Pippa said. 'But if that great huge leggy spider touches me again I'm going to stomp on it, OK?'

There was a tap at the door. 'Goodnight, girls,' Grammy called. 'Sleep tight – hope the bed bugs don't bite!'

''Night!' we all yelled.

'Don't stay up chatting *all* night, will you?' Grammy called with a chuckle.

'We wouldn't dream of it,' Stacy said. 'OK, everyone. Lights out. I want to hear some real loud snoring in, like, *five* minutes.'

We heard Grammy laughing to herself as she went off to the spare bedroom.

'Ow! Fern!' Pippa squeaked. 'Stoppit!'

'It was a bed bug!' Fern laughed. 'I guess it didn't hear what Cindy's Grammy said.'

'Oh, no!' Pippa said. 'A strange power has

taken control of me! It's forcing me to pick up my pillow and hit you over the head with it!'

Whumph! went Pippa's pillow.

'Gurfff!' Fern said through a mouthful of pillow. 'Gurrrf! Nurff!'

'Guys,' Stacy said, sitting up, 'let's not get silly, here. Pillow fights are not exactly sophistica-*guurf*!' Fern's pillow came flying through the air and whacked her right in the mouth.

It took a few minutes for things to calm down again after that.

'Let's play truth or dare,' Stacy said once we'd all remade our wrecked beds and had stopped laughing.

'Nah,' Fern said. 'Let's play murder in the dark.'

'No,' I said. 'Let's *not*.'

'Have you recovered from *Creepshow* yet?' Pippa asked me.

'Of course I have,' I said.

'Then let's tell each other ghost stories,' Pippa said.

'I haven't recovered *that* much,' I said quickly. 'How about we each come up with our very most favourite vacation idea?'

'Me first!' Fern said. 'I'd like to go to Mars.'

'A trip back home, huh?' Stacy said. 'If I had my choice, then I'd really like to –'

'Mooooaaaaaannnnn . . .'

We all went absolutely silent.

'What was that?' Pippa whispered after a few moments.

'It sure wasn't me,' Fern whispered back. 'Stacy? Was that your stomach?'

'Of course not!' Stacy said. She looked at me.

I shook my head.

'Uh . . . what were we talking about?' Pippa asked.

'My . . . favourite . . . vacation . . .' Stacy began. 'I'd like to go on a whale watch up to Vancouver Island. Apparently you can –'

'Moooaaaannnnn. Grooooaaaaannnnnn.'

I nearly freaked out. Even Stacy had gone kind of pale.

Fern sat up in bed. 'For heaven's sake!' she said. 'What the heck *is* that noise?'

I pulled the bed covers up over my face.

I knew what it *sounded* like. It sounded just like the moaning noises we heard over in Joan Ugg's haunted house. Except that this time it sounded like the moaning was coming from somewhere inside my room.

'Who's doing that?' Fern growled. 'If one of you guys is – *urk*!'

'Ohmigosh!' Pippa squealed.

'Sus-sus-sus-Cindy,' Stacy hissed, poking me hard with her elbow. 'Look! *Look!*'

'I don't want to look,' I whimpered.

But I had to look. I lifted one eye over the bed covers.

Pippa and Fern and Stacy were all staring at one point in my room. They all looked totally terrified.

I looked.

Right next to my built-in clothes closet is where I keep my desk. And sitting on my desk is an angle-poise lamp.

And even as I looked with my one eye over the bed covers, my lamp was crawling slowly across the desk – *all by itself*!

I was totally petrified! The lamp moved clear across the desk, shoving other stuff out of the way as it went. The lamp teetered on the edge of the desk for a second or two. Then it toppled over and went crashing down onto the floor.

There was only one explanation.

A horrible, terrible, totally scarifying explanation.

There was a *poltergoose* loose in my room!

14

I was just sucking in a big breath ready to scream the roof right off the house when the chair in front of my desk began to shudder and wobble. At the same moment the moaning noise turned into a petrifying screech of crazy laughter.

The chair wobbled more wildly and pitched over onto its side. The insane laughter turned into a frightful screech of terror.

That did it!

I screamed at the top of my voice.

Stacy yelled as well, and made a wild scramble out of bed and over to the door. Pippa and Fern were right behind her.

Moooooooaaaan! Screeeeech! Grooooooooaaaaaannnn!

'Where's the key! Where's the key!' I heard Stacy hollering.

Then they must have found the key, 'cos the door flew open and the three of them catapulted out into the hallway.

142

I just sat there in bed, screaming and screaming. I couldn't move. The poltergoose was going to get me, and I couldn't move.

Suddenly I was grabbed and dragged out of bed in a tangle of arms and legs and bed clothes. Stacy had rescued me! My best pal in the world had come back into the haunted room and rescued me!

The light suddenly clicked on in the hall. 'What in heaven's name is going on out here?' Grammy stood at the end of the hall in a long white linen night-gown.

'Gug-gog-ghosts!' Pippa squealed, pointing at my room.

'Ghosts?' Grammy laughed. 'What ghosts?'

'In there!' Stacy groaned. 'Honest to gosh.'

Grammy came marching along the corridor.

'It's the ghost of Joan Ugg,' I whimpered. 'We went into her house – and we shouldn't have done – and we made her mad – and she followed us back – and she's in my room – she's a *poltergoose* – she's throwing my stuff around.'

'Is she indeed?' Grammy said. 'We'll see about that!'

She stomped into my room and flicked the light on.

It had all gone very quiet in there.

'So?' Grammy said. 'Where's that pesky ghost? I don't see any ghost.'

Stacy was the first of us to pull herself together. She crept into the room, keeping close to Grammy. 'It could be an invisible ghost,' she said, peeping out from behind Grammy. 'It dragged the lamp across the desk.' The rest of us hung in the doorway, ready to make a run for it at the first groan or at the first sign of any other stuff moving about in there.

'And it knocked the chair over,' Pippa said.

'And it moaned and groaned and cackled and shrieked,' Fern added.

'Did it, now?' Grammy said. 'Well, well. It sounds to me like a very dreadful and fiendish ghost indeed.' She walked over to the chair and stood it up. 'Hmm,' she said. 'I see.'

'What do you see?' Pippa asked.

'I see fishing line,' Grammy said.

'*Fishing line?*' I gasped.

Grammy nodded. 'Fishing line.' She walked over to my closet and pulled the door open. She put her arm in and dragged my clothes aside. 'I think I've found your ghosts, Cindy.'

'It was only a joke,' a small familiar voice squeaked from inside my closet. 'We were only funnin'.'

I stormed in there and stared into the bottom of my closet. Denny and Bob were sitting in there, peering up at us like a pair of mischievous little gnomes.

Grammy started laughing.

Denny and Bob started laughing. 'We got you good!' Bob howled. 'We totally fooled you all!'

'You . . . you . . . you . . .' I was lost for words to express exactly what I was feeling right then.

The guys crowded around and stared at the terrible twins. I guess if Grammy hadn't been there, we'd have yanked the two of them out of the closet and torn them into pieces right there and then and worried about how to dispose of the mess afterwards.

'You have to admit,' Grammy laughed, 'they had you girls on the run!'

'*You Idiots!*' I hollered. I lunged at them. That wiped the smirks off their faces, I can tell you. But Grammy caught hold of me and hugged me up against her so I couldn't move.

'Now, now, Cindy,' she said. 'There's no harm done.'

'It was you two in Joan Ugg's house, wasn't it?' Stacy said.

Denny and Bob nodded and giggled. 'We fooled you good!' Denny said. 'You should have heard yourselves screaming!'

'It was great!' Bob laughed. 'Wait till we tell everyone!'

'Come on out of there,' Grammy said sternly. Denny and Bob slunk out of the closet. I could see the fishing line now. They'd tied one end to the chair and to the lamp, and then they'd threaded the line in through the gap under the closet door so they could yank on it and make it look like stuff was moving on its own.

Denny was carrying a cassette player.

'That's a pretty clever idea with the fishing line,' Pippa said. She looked at the twins. 'Where'd you get it from?'

'We made it up ourselves,' Bob said.

'I don't think so,' Pippa said. She took the cassette player from Denny and flipped it open. 'Aha!' She plucked out the cassette and showed it to us.

Printed on the cassette were the words: *Splaarg The Space Mutant Weekly: The Horror Special Free Fright-tape.*

'That *comic*!' I yelled. 'That's why you hid it from me! It was some kind of dumb horror special.'

'Yeah,' Denny said. 'And it worked, too! We scared you to bits!'

'Why, you . . . !'

'Cindy, calm down, Sweetie,' Grammy said.

She frowned at the twins. 'Now then, boys, you've had your fun. I think it's time we all settled down and got to sleep, don't you?'

Denny poked his tongue out at me. 'We got you good!'

'Denny!' Grammy growled. 'Bed. Both of you! And if I hear another peep out of you before morning, I'll have to give your mom a call and wake her up especially to tell her what's been going on.' Her voice lowered. 'And I think we all know what will happen if I have to do that.'

Yes, indeed – I think we did all know what would happen if Grammy did that. Life as we know it would come to an end in the Spiegel household and we'd all probably be grounded without privileges for the next twenty-five years.

Denny and Bob went back to their own room, but not before Bob pulled a face at me from the hallway.

'If the wind changes, you'll get stuck like that!' I snarled.

'Nyahh! I still won't be as ugly as you!' Bob crowed.

'Bed!' Grammy bellowed. They skedaddled, but there was still a lot of very annoying sniggering and giggling from them.

'Straight to sleep, both of you!' Grammy called.

Their bedroom door slammed.

'Well, now,' Grammy said to us. 'How about you all get yourselves back into bed and simmer down a little, eh?'

'But –'

'The boys were only playing a joke, Cindy,' Grammy said. 'It was just a silly practical joke.' She wagged a finger at me. 'I'm surprised at you for falling for it. You shouldn't be so gullible. Fishing line and cassette tapes!' She chuckled.

We all got back into bed. Grammy sat on the edge of my bed and chatted to us for a little while. She told us a story about mountaineering in Saskatchewan and about how she and Grandpa had seen Bigfoot stomping up a snowy hillside way, way in the distance.

'At least,' she chuckled, 'Grandpa *thought* it was Bigfoot.'

'I don't think Bigfoot exists,' Pippa said. 'There's no such thing, if you ask me!'

Grammy laughed. 'Is this the girl who just ran screaming out of the room because she was being chased by ghosts?' Grammy said.

'I was taken by surprise is all,' Pippa said with dignity. 'I knew deep down that it couldn't be ghosts.'

'Yeah, sure!' Fern said.

Grammy stood up. 'Well, let's not start thinking about that again,' she said. 'I'll be saying goodnight now.' She turned at the door. 'I'm going to sleep with one ear open, girls, and I don't want to hear any little footsteps padding their way along the hallway to the boys' room. Got me?'

'Yes, Grammy,' I said.

'They will have to be killed,' I said. 'Slowly, preferably. Very, very slowly.'

If Grammy had expected us to just turn the light off and go straight to sleep, then Grammy was a little over-hopeful, if you ask me. Sleeping was the very last thing on our minds. Revenge was what we wanted. Lots of revenge. Great huge heaps of lovely revenge. By the time we'd finished with them, those boys were going to wish they'd never heard of *Splaarg The Space Mutant Weekly* comic – and they were especially going to wish that they'd never set eyes on that *Horror Special* issue!

'We should creep along the hall right now,' Fern said. 'We should go right into their room, and we should pound them to mush.'

'No,' Stacy said. 'That's exactly what they'd expect.'

'So, let's not disappoint them,' Pippa said.

'Listen,' Stacy said. 'Let's think this thing through calmly and rationally like the sensible grown-up human beings that we are. Now

149

then: *think* about it. What is our best weapon against Cindy's idiot brothers?'

'A baseball bat,' Fern said.

'No,' Stacy said. 'Not a baseball bat.'

'One of those electric-prod things,' Pippa said. 'Those things that go: *kerzblap!* and the guy falls in a floppy heap on the floor in an instant.'

'*No!*' Stacy said. 'I'm not talking about that kind of thing at all. I'm thinking about the thing between our ears.'

'Our noses?' I said. 'We're going to *sniff* them to death?'

'No!' Stacy groaned. 'Not our noses. Our *brains!*'

'Yes, of course!' Pippa said. 'That's it! We have to defeat them with the power of our brains. Excellent idea, Stacy!'

'I'd rather use a baseball bat,' Fern muttered.

'No,' I said. 'No baseball bats. How would I explain it to Mom and Dad?' I turned to Stacy. 'So,' I said, 'do you have a plan?'

'I think I do,' Stacy said. 'A cunning and sophisticated plan to deal with Dumby and Blob once and for all.' She grinned. 'Huddle up, guys, we don't want to be overheard.'

We all got together on my bed, heads close so Stacy could whisper her plan to us.

'Now,' she said. 'For this plan to work we need the following items: one large jar of maple syrup, half a dozen eggs, Cindy's make-up bag, a really bright lamp and Fern's camera.'

We all stared at her.

She grinned. 'OK, guys, listen up. Here's what we're going to do. First, we have to . . .'

15

The first part of Stacy's cunning and sophisticated plan involved us in a whole lot of hanging around and waiting.

The idea was to use the twins' own sneakiness against them. This was how Stacy figured it:

1. The twins would be expecting us to try to get our own back on them.
2. They would be anticipating a midnight attack on their room.
3. If no attack came, they would start to wonder what we were planning.
4. They would be desperate to know what we were up to.
5. One of them would creep out to check out what was going on.
6. Whoever came creeping along here, would listen at the door to try and hear us plotting and planning.
7. We'd totally fool them with our cunning

and sophisticated plan (Phase One) and then the trap (Phase Two) could be sprung! Ha!

We took it in turns to sit by the door and listen for sneaky creepy footsteps along the hall. The rest of us sat quietly whispering to each other and waiting.

It was over an hour before anything happened.

Pippa was on door-watch.

She gave us the special secret signal that meant 'Monsters on the loose!'

I crept over to the door. Yeah! Sure enough, I could hear little tiny, stealthy padded footsteps. They stopped right outside my door.

Pippa gave me the thumbs up.

It was time for me to make the little play-acting speech that Stacy had come up with.

'OK, guys,' I said. 'It's totally pointless us making a raid on their room tonight – they'll be expecting that. We have to do something that they'd never expect in a million years.'

'Oh, yes,' Pippa said. 'And what is that, Cindy?'

'I call it my Secret Weapon,' I said. I heard a soft thud against the outside of my door. I guess whoever was out there had brought their ear up closer to the woodwork to hear better and had banged their head. Good! I crammed my hands over my mouth to stop myself laughing.

'Your *Secret Weapon*, Cindy?' Pippa acted (very badly, if you ask me). 'What is *that*, Cindy?'

'I can't tell you right now,' I said. 'But it's something I've been storing away in the cellar for just such an emergency situation as we are in right now. It will finish those twins off for ever! I'll tell you what we're going to do, guys. First thing in the morning, I'll go down to the cellar, and I'll go get the Secret Weapon, which is hidden away right at the back behind some old rolls of carpet. And when we have the Secret Weapon, I'll be able to deal with my horrid little brothers once and for all. No kidding, I will!'

'That sounds like a great idea, Cindy,' Pippa said, her mouth close to our side of the door. 'In the meantime, I think it would be a good idea for us to get some sleep right now.'

'I agree,' I said. 'Goodnight, Pippa.'

'Goodnight, Cindy,' Pippa said. 'Goodnight, Fern. Goodnight, Stacy.'

'Goodnight, Pippa,' said Fern. 'Goodnight, Cindy. Goodnight, Stacy.'

'Goodnight, Fern,' Stacy said. 'Goodnight, Pippa. Goodnight, Cindy.'

'Goodnight, Stacy,' I said. 'Goodnight, Fern.' I did a really big theatrical yawn. '*Ya-a-a-a-w-w-w-wn!*'

Not one of us said another word or made a move.

We just kept totally still and silent and *listened.*

A few seconds later I heard someone creeping back along the hallway.

Stacy gave me the thumbs up.

But would they fall for it?

To be honest, a person would have to be pretty dumb to believe I had a Secret Weapon stashed away in the cellar. Pretty darned dumb! As dumb as donkeys!

'Pippa?' I whispered.

'Uh-huh?'

'That was the worst piece of acting I've ever heard,' I said. 'It's a good thing the twins are dumb as donkeys.'

'Shhhh!' Stacy hissed. 'Listen.'

We all crammed our ears up against the door.

'Aha!' Stacy whispered.

We could just hear whispering voices out in the hall. And then we heard the faint creaking of two sets of feet sneaking down the stairs.

'They went for it!' Fern chuckled. She grinned at us. 'It's show time, folks!'

We gave it a few seconds, and then I quietly opened the door. I heard the click downstairs of someone opening the cellar door. Excellent!

Clutching my make-up bag, I snuck out into the hallway. Fern came next, carrying her camera. Pippa was third, she was toting my angle-poise lamp. The plan was that Stacy would make a diversion into the kitchen to fetch the maple syrup and the eggs.

We slid noiselessly down the stairs.

The cellar door was open a fraction and the light had been put on. Stacy crept off to the kitchen while the rest of us waited.

I put my ear to the gap in the door. I could hear the twins muttering to one another down there. Poor unsuspecting goofs!

Stacy joined us again with a carton of eggs and a brand-new two-litre bottle of really thick and gooey maple syrup.

We looked at one another.

'Let's go,' Stacy said.

We crept through the door and tiptoed down the cellar steps. Pippa closed the door tight and then sat on the stairs – barring the way out.

I led the way down.

The twins were rooting around in the back of the cellar. They didn't have the least idea of what was about to hit them.

'Well, hello, boys,' I said. 'Fancy meeting you two down here.'

They spun around with shocked, stunned looks on their faces. It was perfect! Perfectly perfect, to quote a really good pal of mine. Super-extra-first-class *perfectly* perfect!

I grinned at them. 'Welcome to your worst nightmare!'

'Ever get the feeling you've been *had*?' Stacy asked.

Denny's eyes narrowed. 'I'm not scared of you. You won't do anything to us. You wouldn't dare.'

He came towards us, like he meant to bust right past.

Fern stepped in front of him. He tried to side-step her, but she spread her arms.

'Stacy, the eggs, please,' Fern growled, giving Denny her most ferocious boy-eating look.

Stacy handed her the egg carton. Fern opened it and took out an egg. Denny watched her warily. 'Ever seen my version of the great egg trick?' Fern said, flipping the egg in her hand. 'All I require is one small pest and half a dozen raw eggs.'

She advanced on him. Denny backed away. And without Denny to lead the way, Bob sure wasn't going anywhere.

'What do you want?' Denny asked.

'I want to spend some quality time with my little brothers,' I said. 'That's all I want.' I looked at them and shook my head. 'Don't take offence, guys, but I think the pair of you could use a little help with your personal grooming.'

I put my make-up bag on the workbench down there and unzipped it. Denny and Bob stared at the bag. I think they were beginning to guess what we had in mind.

'I'll yell and Grammy will come,' Denny said.

'Possibly,' Fern growled. 'But by the time she gets here you'll be wearing three eggs and half a jar of maple syrup each.' She smiled. 'You'd be amazed how much maple syrup I could pour down inside the back of your pyjamas before your grammy rescued you.' She nodded cheerfully. 'You really would!'

'You wouldn't dare,' Denny said.

'Oh, yes I would,' Fern said. She took the jar from Stacy and unscrewed the lid. She moved towards the boys, lifting the jar and tilting it. 'I'd do it, boys, and I'd *love* it. Just give me the excuse.'

'We could get the Secret Weapon,' Bob muttered to Denny. He pointed to the rolls of carpets up against the wall.

'There isn't no secret weapon, dummy,' Denny said.

'You catch on fast,' Stacy laughed.

'So, what's it to be, boys?' I asked totally reasonably. 'Are you going to sit still for a really good make-over, or do we leave you to Fern?' I looked at them. 'Now, you *know* you deserve some kind of punishment for all those ghost stunts you pulled on us. I'm letting you off lightly, really.' I gave them a really hard look. 'Or do you want me to go away right now and let you loose and spend the next few days coming up with something *really* nasty?'

The boys looked at my make-up bag. Then they looked at one another. Then they looked at Fern. Fern grinned and waved the eggs and the open syrup jar at them.

'Bob first!' Denny said.

'*No!!*' Bob howled. 'It was all Denny's idea! I didn't do nuffin'. I didn't even go to that house with him. And I didn't go upstairs and make the creaking noises while he played the tape and made the chair move with the fishing line. It was all him! I didn't do it! I wasn't even *there*!'

'You were, too, you big fibber!' Denny exclaimed.

'Was not!'

'Woz!'

'Wozzn't!'

'Boys, chill out,' I said. 'There's no need for anyone to fall out over this.' I reached into my make-up bag and pulled out my Scarlet Sunburst lipstick. (Mom doesn't let me leave the house with make-up on, but she's OK with me experimenting indoors – and I do love to experiment with make-up.)

I twirled the stick so the red lipstick poked out of the top. I held it out and headed towards the boys.

This was going to be a total riot!

We found a couple of stools for them to sit on. Pippa plugged in the lamp so we had a good bright light to work by. And then we got down to it. With a vengeance! The twins squirmed and wriggled and screwed up their faces, but we were totally ruthless with them. Well, come on – they deserved it!

But, do you know something: I think those ungrateful little brothers of mine didn't appreciate all the work the four of us did on them! Not one little bit, they didn't! Can you beat that? We worked like crazy to give them the very best make-over that we could, and not once did they say 'Thank you, Stacy,' or 'That looks really great, Cindy,' or 'Nice work, Pippa,' even though Fern was constantly showing them how good they were looking in my make-up mirror.

'There's not a whole lot I can do with your hair, boys,' I explained while I tried to brush Denny's spiky thatch into interesting and new shapes. 'But I think a few grips here and there will help. Stacy? Pass me a few of those lovely butterfly grips. Oh and some ribbons, too, please.'

'Grgrrurrgh . . .' Denny muttered.

'Sorry? Did you say something?'

'No.'

'Good.'

Then there was:

'Bob, you really have to keep still right now – it's kind of tricky putting mascara on right, and you'll get the brush in your eye if you keep squirming around like that.'

'Owww!'

'There! Told you so!'

And there was:

'Which shade of blusher goes best with your skin tones, Denny? Peach Blossom or Shocking Pink? What do you say? You don't know? Well, in that case I think I'll give the Shocking Pink a try.'

And finally, after half an hour's solid work:

'There! You're both finished!'

We stepped back to admire our handiwork.

It was no good trying to keep straight faces – we all fell about laughing *instantly*. It wasn't just all the make-up and hair grips and ribbons that cracked us up – it was the expressions on Denny and Bob's faces!

They sat there glowering at us with great wads of lippy and eyeliner and mascara and blusher and spangly glitter stars all over their miserable sulky kissers! It was priceless!

'You know something,' Stacy said. 'I think they'd make really really pretty little girls.' She held the mirror up for them. 'What do *you* think?'

'We should rename them Debbie and Babs,' Pippa shrieked.

'Can we go now?' Denny muttered. Not at *all* amused.

'What do you think, guys?' I asked. 'Should we let them go now?'

'I think so,' Stacy laughed. 'They're as gorgeous as they're going to get.'

Seething with humiliation, the twins got up off the stools and headed for the stairs.

'Oh! Wait!' I said. 'We're forgetting something! We should preserve this moment for posterity! Fern? Your camera, please.'

Fern whipped out her camera and before the boys could make a move, she'd snapped them both.

The picture came sliding out of its slot.

'Perfect!' I said. The twins were beautifully framed in the picture – they hadn't even had time to put their hands up over their faces.

'They look so cute,' Pippa crooned.

Denny made a snatch for the picture, but I held it up out of reach.

'Do you know what this picture is?' I said to the boys. 'It's my Secret Weapon! If you two ever annoy me or irritate me or play any of your stupid tricks on me ever again – for the rest of your lives – I'm going to go along to the photography store in the mall – and I'm going to ask them to make me a dozen poster-sized blow-ups of this picture – and I'm going to pin them up all over town, so that *everyone* can see how pretty you look.' I grinned at them. 'Get the picture?'

'Grunnf,' Denny grunted.

'I'm sorry,' I said. 'I didn't quite catch that.'

'Yes,' Denny muttered. 'Are you going to let us go now?'

'Sure thing,' I said with a big smile. 'Off you go! And mind you don't get make-up all over your pillows!'

They zipped up the cellar stairs like a pair of made-over rockets.

The four of us grinned at one another.

We did a high-five and burst out laughing.

Well, to cut a long story short, my dear brothers spent over an hour in the bathroom that night before they managed to scrape all the make-up off their faces.

We hardly saw anything of them the next morning. They seemed to be really busy up in their room for some reason, so the four of us were able to watch another of Fern's videos before the guys had to go home.

Grammy gave me some curious looks during the day – almost like she suspected that something had happened between the four of us and the twins; but she never said anything, and the twins sure never breathed a word.

So long as I have that picture hidden away safe in my room, I have a real hold over Denny and Bob. And if they start annoying me, all I'll have to do is to say 'make-over time' to them, and they'll be as good as gold.

Now that's what I call girl power!

Big sister power!

Yeah! Cindy for ever!

P.S.

Rats! Ratsratsrats!

You're not going to *believe* this!

The sneaky little beasts sneaked into my room and sneaked around in there until they sneakily found the picture!

I guess we're evens again, now.

Darn!

Stacy certainly gets herself into some sticky situations. In the next great book in the series, she needs help – from her sister and arch enemy, Amanda – aargh! Here's a sneak preview . . .

Sister Switch

RRRRRRRIIIIINNNNNNGGGGGGGGG!

Have you ever seen an entire class jump two feet into the air? Until that alarm clock went off it had been totally quiet in our classroom. The only sound you could hear was the scratching of pens on paper and the occasional groan as someone got to a question straight out of their nightmares.

'What on earth is going on?' Ms Fenwick bounded up out of her seat as though it had suddenly bitten her.

'Ow! Owowowowow!' Betsy Jane Garside was sitting right in front of me and she started howling in pain because she'd jabbed her pencil in her eye when the alarm clock had gone off.

We were in the middle of a maths test. I was on Question Twelve. These two guys were travelling towards each other on trains. One of them had left Town A at six o'clock in the morning and was travelling east at eighty five miles an hour. The other guy had left Town B at eight o'clock and was going west at seventy miles an hour. The towns were five hundred miles apart and we were supposed to figure out where and when the two guys would meet. If you ask me, they could have saved everyone a whole lot of trouble if they'd just *called* each other on the phone.

I was sitting there with my pencil in my mouth, gazing out of the window and imagining these two trains charging towards each other. But the question didn't mention whether they were on the same track. If they *were* on the same track, then I was thinking that the question should really read: *Where and at what time will the two trains crash into each other?*

I guess you're not supposed to wonder about stuff like that in the middle of a maths test. And another thing that's not supposed to happen in the middle of a maths test is for an alarm clock to go off in someone's bag.

'It's a fire drill!' Larry Franco shouted. 'We should evacuate the building!'

'It's not a fire drill,' Ms Fenwick said. She came swooping up the row where I was sitting and homed in on my bag.

RRRRRRIIIIIINNNNNNGGGGG!

'Stacy, could you please put a stop to that infernal *noise!*' Ms Fenwick said.

That's me: Stacy Allen, once an ordinary ten-year-old student in Four Corners, Indiana. Now, the cause of infernal noises in the middle of a maths test.

'Betsy Jane, what were you yelling about?' Ms Fenwick asked.

'I jabbed my pencil in my eye!' Betsy Jane wailed.

While Ms Fenwick examined Betsy Jane's eye, I hauled my bag up onto my desk and rummaged through my stuff in search of the ringing alarm clock.

There it was. Right at the bottom. It got even louder as I pulled it out and jerked down the lever to shut it off.

'*Thank* you,' Ms Fenwick said. 'Quiet, everyone, please!'

The whole class was talking now and, out of Ms Fenwick's eyesight, a few kids were swapping answers.

Ms Fenwick's eagle-eyes moved around the class and everyone went quiet.

'Well, Stacy?' she said, looking at the alarm clock and then looking at me. 'Would you like to explain why you thought it was a good idea to bring an alarm clock to class?'

Good question.

But did I have a good answer? I sure did, but not one I could tell Ms Fenwick. I knew *exactly* how that alarm clock got into my bag. And it was nothing to do with me, I can tell you that. I *knew* who put it there, and I knew why.

'I must have put it in there by accident,' I said to Ms Fenwick. 'Things like that happen when you're in a hurry,' I added. I looked at my friend Cindy. 'Don't they?'

Cindy gave me a blank look for a second then nodded in agreement. 'They sure do,' she said. 'Last week I brought a tube of toothpaste into school by mistake. I don't know how it got in my bag because I hadn't taken my bag into the bathroom at all that morning.'

'Aliens, I guess,' said Fern, who was sitting right behind us. Just recently Fern has started blaming aliens for anything strange that happens.

A tube of toothpaste appears in your school bag? *Aliens!*

An alarm clock goes off in the middle of a maths test? You got it: *Aliens!*

Bug-eyed monsters from Venus. Except that the bug-eyed monster who put the alarm clock in my bag wasn't from Venus. She was from the bedroom down the hall from mine. It was my big, airheaded bimbo of a sister, Amanda!

I knew *why*. It was her idea of a really great way of getting back at me for slipping one of Sam's pacifiers in with her cheerleading stuff the day before.

But I only did that to pay her back for pinning a *Kick Me* sign onto the back of my sweater the day before that. She *started* it!

Honest, she did! OK, so the *Kick Me* note was to get back at me for taking the laces out of her sneakers. But what would you do if your sister doctored your toothpaste with soap so you came screaming out of the bathroom foaming at the mouth like you had *rabies*?

I'll be honest with you: I don't really remember *who* started all this revenge stuff. But I was pretty determined about who was going to *finish* it.

Me, that's who.

My first reaction was to hunt Amanda down after class and stuff the alarm clock right down her throat. But no; that wouldn't be *nearly* bad enough. What I needed to come up with was something so *sneaky*, so *diabolically* clever that people in our school would be talking about it in twenty years' time.

It would be known as *The Great Revenge*. The day when Stacy finally won over her big sister! Brain over brawn. Not that Amanda's especially brawny, except between the ears. The real problem is that she's a couple of years older than me and behaves like she knows *everything*.

I'll tell you, you could write down everything Amanda knows on the back of a postage stamp, and still leave room for the Gettysburg Address.

Anyway, Ms Fenwick got everyone settled down again and we finished the maths test without anything going off in anyone else's bag. I guess no one else in my class has a crazy older sister like I do.

'Amanda's gone too far this time,' I told my three best friends as we headed back to my house after school. 'I'm going to have to *kill* her. It's the only way the rest of my life is going to be worth living.'